First of all, this book is dedicated to my family for putting up with my continued existence.

To Professor Sir Terry Pratchett, for inspiring me to write.

And last, but not least, to Griffin, Logan, Cody, and that freshman kid whose name I can never remember, for being the best friends I've ever had. I am unsure as to if I should include one other in this list, as by the time this book comes out he will have emerged from his chrysalis as a fully-fledged weaboo, flying off to join his kin in Glorious Nippon. However, on the off chance he has not yet begun to pupate, this book is also dedicated to Spencer. In the event that he has completed metamorphosis, I wish him luck in his servitude to the Lords of Outer Night, and beseech him to bring a message to Narutotep, the Conspicuous Chaos:

Uguũ.

Table of Contents

Prologue

Let us look at this world from above, from the view of the gods. Take in the green of the forests and the grey of the mountains. Then forget about everything I just said and zoom in on a speck of nothing.

Said little speck is theoretically a town, although *heap* or perhaps *pile* would be a better word. The only right angles visible are those on the imperial garrison, an impressive fortification wrought by goblin day laborers during the elder time of last Tuesday from a single sack of concrete shielded via stoutest Masonite. In front, there is a soldier pacing back and forth, red and black armor gleaming in the sunlight. Her name is Travia Praecantator and she has five minutes to live.

Step. Step. Step.

Four minutes.

As she paced, Travia looked back on her past and the events that brought her to this backwater town.

Step. Step. Step.

Three minutes.

Six years ago, just one week after her thirteenth birthday, things had been radically different. She was apprenticed to the wizard Sinyeï. Every day she got up, awakened the other apprentice as rudely as possible, pulled some food out of the Aether, and helped her master with research until it was time to return to bed. That is, every day until things changed.

Step. Step. Step.

Two minutes.

On that fateful morning, she awoke to the smell of burning flesh. Quickly rushing over to a window, she looked out and saw the town in flames. Directly underneath, she saw her master fighting off what seemed to be the entire imperial army. It didn't go well for him.

Step. Step. Step.

One minute.

Panicking, she ran into his laboratory and activated the wand of teleport he kept there, appearing in a forest some fifty miles away. Using her magical skills to survive, she formulated a plan. Once she was of age, she would join the imperial army and work her way up. Then, the real fun would begin.

Step. Step. Step.

Thirty seconds.

All she had to do would be to find a local cell of the resistance, and then she could give them whatever information came her way. Passwords, troop movements, tactics, everything.

Step. Step. Step.

Five seconds.

Four seconds.

Three.

Two.

One.

Now.

There was the crack of a spark, and the whoosh of flame. Travia didn't even have time to scream before her skin reached temperatures high enough to melt lead. At least it was quick. That's more than the people inside would get.

5

Chapter 1
They All Met In a Cliché

They all met in a jail cell. The cunning wizard, the ~~sneaky thief~~ loveable rogue, the powerful fighter, and the surly dwarf who resented people that confuse his race and profession. When Magus's hangover had finally worn off, he looked up and saw a group of ~~clichés~~ people, who conveniently filled the above descriptions.

In the corner, there was a leathery skinned kobold that appeared to have not had a good meal in some time. His beady little eyes flicked back and forth whenever anyone moved and his forked tongue constantly flitted in and out, tasting the air. Sitting on the wooden cot was a blue-eyed dwarf. His beard was so large that no other features on his face could be made out, but it was not ragged like a thistle patch, but well taken care of, like a hedge, or possibly some kind of bonsai tree. He was wearing flowing robes of purple silk, coated with hanging rings and menacing spikes, but they were stained and tattered, making it obvious their owner had fallen upon hard times. Standing in the corner there was a tall, Nordic looking woman with the stance of a fighter.

At this point, normally I would go on about naked blades and chainmail bikinis while talking to the cover artist until whoever was reading the book would have to go lie down, but sadly, such things are rather impractical in combat. Anyone who goes into a melee wearing metal underwear deserves it when their blood ends up decorating the walls, and thus the warrior was simply wearing serviceable chain mail over some of the itchy garments most peasants call clothes. The cell itself was spartan, with the bar-and-stone motif that has been used to keep people in one place since the beginning of time.

After the round of introductions, Magus learned that the dwarf was named Petrov, the kobold was named Ibn-Abda, and the woman was named Aeringaner... Eringorner... Araran... Eowin... Look, can I just call you Erin?

"No. My name is Æringunnr Geirssdóttir."

How about Kelly? That's a nice name.

"No. Æringunnr."

But I can't pronounce that! You know what, screw this. It's not like you can do anything to stop me. Anyway, after a conversation with Erin—

"Æringunnr."

Whatever. Anyway, after a conversation and an inspection of some napkins he had scribbled on while drunk, Magus discovered that not only had he sworn to avenge himself upon the empire for something or other, but that the people before him had been drunk enough to think swearing loyalty to him was a good idea.

Elated by this revelation, Magus got up, and walked out to a new dawn. Or at least, he would have if there weren't all those bars and things in the way.

After a bit more conversation, they realized one of them must have done something while drunk, as all of them had been in the tavern when it burned down, with the exception of Abda, who was in for Grand Theft Onion. While they were arguing about whose fault it was that they were in trouble, the warden, a portly man with red cheeks and an expression of indifference, walked up with a couple of nameless, redshirt guards and managed to cuff our heroes and drag them out before anyone noticed his existence.

"*Yebut!*" Petrov said. "Look at trouble you've gotten us into!"

"*Me?*" replied Magus. "*You* were the one with the vodka! How else do you think that place got burned down?"

"You did it!" shouted Petrov.

"*How?!*" Magus said. "Do you think I just waved my fingers and blew the place up with magic?!"

7

"*Da*. You're vizard. Zat's what vizards do," replied Petrov.

"Well played, dwarf. Well played."

As the argument raged, the warden and guards dragged them roughly along until they reached the office of the captain of the guard. The guard in front respectfully opened the door, and the warden took them in and pushed them down into some chairs in front of the commander's desk. The commander, a grizzled old man with a graying mustache, shuffled some of the strata of paperwork on his desk and gave Magus a sidelong look.

"Well, well, well. Magus. Magus Breeman. I hope you realize how hard you are making my life," he said. "Five people are dead because of you."

Suddenly, the last scraps of the hangover faded and all of a sudden, Magus remembered everything.

He was Magus, apprentice to the wizard Sinyeĭ. One day, just a few months after his fourteenth birthday, he'd gone out to chop firewood. In the forest he met a man wearing a suit with a voice like a sword on a grindstone. The man offered to take Magus with him, claiming it was the call to adventure. Magus refused. He still remembered the man's words before parting: "THE CALL KNOWS WHERE YOU LIVE."

When he returned to town, everything was aflame, burned down by the Imperial army. His master, with his last words, passed his staff along to Magus and then died right before revealing something important about Magus's parents that would probably take years for Magus to figure out on his own. He spent the next twelve years in solitude, preparing for his revenge.

He knew he would need allies, so he got them the way any adventurer would. He put on a cloak and sat in the corner of the bar looking into his beer. They all met in that tavern. Save the town, they had figured, kill the imperial oppressors, and tear down the flag that had appeared so often in Magus's nightmares. Perhaps they should have considered that just because the troops were the enemy did not mean they had no family.

The party attacked the garrison and slaughtered the inhabitants. Afterward they came out, burned the flag Magus had seen with hatred ever since that day twelve years ago, and announced to the townspeople that they were free. They had expected congratulation and praise, not hateful looks and tears. They drank that night in an attempt to forget what had happened.

While they were in a helpless, drunken stupor, the townspeople attacked. Magus knew he was lucky that the remains of law enforcement stopped them from being lynched on the spot. However, he had no clue where they were now or how they'd gotten there.

"Now then, if you're done with your part of the exposition," said the commander, "I'll fill in the blanks for you." He coughed, and when he spoke again it was in an odd, foreboding voice. "*While you were unconscious, the remaining guards—*"

Mid-sentence, the commander had a coughing fit. When he regained his voice he said, "That dramatic voice really hurts the throat. I'm telling the rest the normal way. Anyway, you were loaded up on a cart and brought over here to the capital of the barony. You'll be jailed for a while, and after that you'll get a trial if there's any lawyer who can plead for you with a straight face. A few days later we'll carry out your executions and everyone else can live happily ever after."

"Not jail! I'm too pretty for jail!"

"Shut up, Magus." the commander ordered. "Despite popular belief, none of our inmates are named Hump and weigh six hundred pounds. We do have a five hundred-pound inmate named Hump, but he's already got a cellmate. *Sergeant!*"

"Yes sir?" said the portly warden as he walked into the room.

"Take the inmates down to the cells. And, Fred, I know they've done horrible things, but we're doing this by the book, so make sure they don't fall down the stairs or anything."

"Yessir."

The mortally obese sergeant walked them down to a cell and rudely shoved them in, slamming the door with a very final clang. Their surroundings were dismal, with several wooden cots and a urine encrusted, malodorous chamber pot which, after one slosh, would cause any sane man to allow his bowels to explode. Naturally, the bottom of the pot had a hole in in it. Below was a spreading brown stain on the floor.

"Hey, you! Guard!" shouted Abda. "Any chance of you walking in arm's reach with the keys on a big dangly ring attached to your belt?"

"That's never gonna happen," said the guard. "Sarge keeps the only set locked up in his desk."

"Let me try," said Petrov. "I nobility. I know how zis goes. *Allo!* Guard! How much for you get us out?"

"Figure out how much money you have. Then double it."

"I hate you, too."

"Oh, you don't hate me just yet. But you will. Believe me, you will."

Petrov turned to look forlornly at the group. "I sorry Magus. Nothing more I can do. This is a very honest *oblat*."

The group waited for a few minutes until suddenly, Abda jumped up and rushed over to the wall.

"Vhat's this?" He pushed several unrelated rocks, then stood expectantly.

"Well? What was it?" said Magus.

"Nothing. I was joking." The kobold sounded more sullen when he added, "We're all going to die."

"Well, since we're all about to die," said Magus, turning toward Aran—Aarawen—She Who Can Not Be Pronounced with a grin, "we might as well—"

"Try something and I pull your spleen out through your throat."

"Shutting up."

Magus sat down on his cot to sleep, but jumped back up shouting, "Guys, I know how we can escape!"

Everyone else just glared at him. She Who Can Not Be Pronounced said, "Look, the joke wasn't funny when Abda did it, and it isn't funny now."

"No, seriously this time! Quick, everyone check under the beds!"

"What, are you afraid of there being monsters under them?"

"Yes, but that's not important right now! Something I remember reading in the imperial building regulations! There has to be at least one emergency exit in any given room!"

"You read those?"

"I was bored, okay? Anyway, what's under the beds?"

"Nothing here," said Petrov.

"There's a portal to R'lyh underneath mine but I think it would be best if we leave it shut," said Abda.

"And there's an entrance to the sewers under mine!" said... Look, do you have anything more pronounceable I can call you?

"My friends call me Ærin."

...said Ærin.

"You are not my friend."

Look, I'm running out of options here. It's either Ærin or Patsy.

"Ærin it is."

"Look," said Magus, "can we get going here? There's not much time before the guards realize what's going on."

"What do you mean by that?" responded Ærin. "This is a fantasy setting. The cops are called insecurity guards for a reason. There's one question during the interview and it's 'what is your name.' If you get it wrong, you're hired."

"Still best not take risks," said Petrov.

Magus walked over to the cot, plugged his nose, and jumped into a liquid that if called mud would offend thousands of perfectly innocent swamps. Two splashes behind him announced that the rest had jumped in as well. However, all was not well. He had three companions. He turned around in the ooze, took stock of his companions, and said, "Where's Petrov?"

"Up here, manling!"

Magus looked up in fear of a celling crawling monster with Petrov in its grip. Instead he saw Petrov clinging to the celling by his beard.

"What...?" sputtered Magus. "How...?"

"Well," said Petrov, "vhat did you zink beard was for? Decoration?"

"Yes..."

"I can't believe you get shocked over such a little thing," said Ærin. "If you weren't a wizard, I'd think you were some kind of plot-important orphan raised by a bunch of hillbillies out in the sticks."

"Why can't I be?" said Magus. "I was adopted by a wizard after my parents died, and he was killed right before announcing a prophetic revelation. It fits the cliché perfectly!"

"Because you're a wizard!" said Ærin. "Wizards make prophesies; they don't fulfill them."

"Well then, maybe it's time for a change!"

Magus walked onward toward the light at the end of the tunnel, filled with hope, leaving the sewer for a better—or at least less smelly—future.

Or at least he would if it weren't for all the bars and things. Again. For some unknown reason there were bars over the place where the pipe drained out in one of the tributaries of the river Ankh.

"Dammit!" swore Magus. "Who in their right mind puts bars on the exit of a sewer? Are they afraid of the smell escaping! Don't want it in their nice disgusting river?"

"You vizzard," said Petrov. "Can't you just melt zem?"

"Yeah, but that's not the point. Anyway, stand back. I'm going to hit it with a blob of acid." Magus began to wave his hands, arcane energy trailing them, illuminating the walls with a purple glow. Then, looking suitably impressive, he began to chant in a mysterious language.

"ERO ACCOMMO HOSPES MIHI CREDE STURM," he said. *"NON LECTUS PARO IGNE ORUM, ET SI VENENUM BENE."*

A green haze appeared over the bars.

"AMOR SUM MULIER PULCHRA ET NESCIEBAM. MODO NOSTRAM FORTUNAM."

The bars began to sizzle.

"PECCAVI SATIS CUM MUNDO. DOCENTES A MAGICA ERIT KENDER DAMNATIONEM."

Little droplets of molten metal began to ooze off the bars.

"NEQUE ENIM FABULA FAIRY TIMET?"

And with that last eldritch phrase, the bars dissolved until there was a hole in them big enough to walk through. Magus stepped through, wading out into the river, and the rest of the party followed.

"Now what?" said Ærin as they climbed onto the nearby docks.

"Well, we go get new weapons, obviously." responded Magus.

"Yes, but they took all my money."

"And?" asked Magus. "Why else do we have Abda with us? You can't have a proper adventuring party without a thief."

"I take offense at that!" replied Abda. "I'm not a thief, I'm a rogue!"

"You pick peoples' pockets," said Magus.

"That's not stealing, that's a public service. I'm cleaning them! Think of how cluttered they would get if I wasn't here to help."

"Well, go help someone then!"

They watched as Abda tried to take peoples' wallets, but somehow everyone knew when he was coming.

"I'm sorry guys, but somehow they know when I'm coming!" said Abda, nicely recapping. "Maybe everyone in the city is psychic."

"Or it might be because they can smell you coming from a mile away," said Ærin. "Let's face it. After that trip in the sewers, we stink."

"Ha! You humans soft," interjected Petrov. "This is nothing compared to life in old country! Back in Boïneudalos', floors were coated with noxious secretions. Just touch them and your legs rot off. When goblins invaded, we didn't wear armor because nothing was more dangerous than taking clothes off to put armor on!"

"Good for you," said Magus. "Now if you'll excuse us, we soft humans are off to go see if we can find some water."

Suddenly, upon hearing Magus proclaim their search, Ærin burst into laughter. "Water! Clean water! In a city! What are you, some kind of an idiot? You may not be a plot-important orphan but you were definitely raised by hillbillies."

"I was raised by a wizard!" said Magus. "He had a tower and everything. It was like... three stories tall!"

"Look around you!" shouted Ærin. "All the houses here are around three stories tall!"

"How does zis even relate to what we were talking about?" interjected Petrov.

"What?" said Ærin. "Oh yes, the water. This is a city. There's so much dumped in the river you can walk across it. It takes so much time to boil water you're lucky there's any for drinking!"

"Look," said Magus, as he walked over to an elderly lady wearing expensive clothes a permanent grimace. "Everyone here's clean. There's got to be bathhouses or something. I'll ask her for directions."

"Hello," said Magus. "My companions and I have found ourselves in dire straits, and would be very appreciative of your help. Can you direct us to the bathhouses?"

15

"Yes," said the old lady. "I can."

Time passed.

"*Well?*" said Magus impatiently.

"What do you mean, '*well?*'" asked the lady. "You asked whether I *could,* not whether I *would.* I know what you meant, but I don't see any reason to help you."

"How about in the name of common decency?" said Magus, quickly becoming enraged.

"Of course not," said the lady. "Decency is common, and thus found in commoners. I'm an objectivist, and we're rare. Scum like you sit around in the street and wait for someone to help you, whereas we build industries with our bare hands."

"Really?" said Magus sarcastically. "All by yourself?"

"Yes," said the old woman. "Technically we employ people to build them, but they don't have a six-figure salary, so they don't count as humans. Now, why don't you get out of my way, and learn not to be cheeky to your betters."

Magus's eyes narrowed. "No," he said, as a ball of eldritch balefire materialized in the palm of his curled hand. "Perhaps you are different from other people, but you know what? I'm willing to bet you burn the same."

****

"...One thousand ninety eight, one thousand ninety-nine... eleven hundred," said Magus as he went through the coin purse of the recently deceased. "I think we have enough money to rearm ourselves. According to the map, there's a discount magic item shop nearby."

After a bit of travel, our heroes arrived at a shop which—inexplicably— had a picture of a cat on its sign. The store looked unfrequented, unlike the shops to either side of it. Inside, there was dust everywhere. The weapons were cluttered together in umbrella stands, with labels like, "Fifty percent off!" or "GREAT BUY!!!!" which had not been changed for some time. Suits of armor hung from the walls, ranging from a chain hauberk to a full set of plate mail. There was no light other than what came in from the windows, and although the merchandise had been painstakingly maintained, it looked like no one had been in the store for a very long time.

Ærin took a broadsword out of a bin, swung it around a bit and said, "This one. This one's mine."

"Why can't we just steal weapons, too?" asked Abda.

"Because," said Magus, "any wizard capable of making magic items would be able to fireball anyone who tries to steal them."

"Let's go find the counter," said Abda. "I'm not sure about you, but I'm rather attached to my organs and would really dislike losing them."

Out of nowhere came a bald, stunted and gray bearded apparition in blue robes and a black cape. The specter walked up to the party before looking at Petrov.

"*Allo, privet!*"

"*Allo!*" responded Petrov.

"Wait," said Magus. He looked at Petrov. "Your last name is Privet?"

The two dwarfs looked at Magus and burst into laughter.

"No, no," said Petrov after recovering. "*Privet* is what you say when you meet someone."

"And the *allo* thing?"

"Zat means 'Hello,'" replied the dwarf.

Magus stared at Petrov for a moment, then decided to drop it.

"Anyway," he said to the dwarven shopkeep. "We'd like to buy this and a couple daggers."

"And a battle axe!" said Petrov.

"Really?" said the shopkeep, hope rising in his eyes. "Bless you!"

"Why are there no other customers?" asked Ærin. "Your weapons are very well made."

"Because," said the shopkeep, "the adventurers' guild is boycotting me. Said my goods veren't up to snuff. Vhat's worse, it's not because of their quality, it's because of their effect. That sword you hold turns its victim's internal organs into kittens! Sure, it doesn't look as cool as a flaming sword, but it has a far more useful effect! I haven't had any customers in months! Hell, buy a breastplate with it, and I'll throw in a shield for free!"

"All right," said Ærin. "Do you have them in red?"

Chapter 2
When You're Tired of Civilization, You're Tired of Living in Ankle-Deep Shit.

"All right," said the shopkeep. "So that's one breastplate of temperature resistance, one shield, one sword of kitten transmutation, two punching daggers, and one knife with squiggly runes engraved on it. Will that be all?"

"There's also a battle axe!" interjected Petrov. "Don't forget the battle axe!"

"Ah yes. And one battle axe. That will be one hundred lords, please."

"Lords?" asked Magus.

"The steel coins."

"Oh, sure. Here you go."

Magus handed over the money, but when they walked out of the shop a group of men carrying instrument cases and pretending to be bards walked over. Since all of them were over six feet tall and wearing cheap suits, their disguises weren't very convincing.

The largest of them, a hulking giant with one eye, picked up Magus by the hem of his robe and said "I dot Midder Bromad made it clear dat nobody was to buy nuffen 'ere."

"Sorry!" Magus squeaked.

"Youz gonna die, mage."

Magus turned to the party and squeaked, "Help!"

"I might as well," said Ærin. "I was looking forward to seeing what this sword could do."

Ærin poked the thug with her new sword and a droplet of blood dripped down it.

"Was that supposed to 'urt?" said the thug.

Or at least that was probably what he had been meaning to say. It changed into agonized screams halfway through. He quickly dropped Magus in order to writhe in agony properly.

After a while, his thrashing stilled, and there was a scratching sound. Then a claw punctured his abdomen from the inside. The small hole was widened and soon, out came a litter of tabby kittens, coated in blood and gore, along with a black cat that tunneled its way out of the thug's skull via an eye socket.

The other thugs watched in surprise for a bit before opening up their instrument cases. *Surprise, surprise!* They weren't keeping instruments in them.

While Magus vainly attempted out of melee range, Ærin and Petrov leapt into the fray. The nameless thugs attacked, but they were obviously outclassed. Ærin feinted left and right, stabbing them every time. Arms, legs and kittens were scattered everywhere. When Magus finally gave up on running and reduced one of the remaining thugs to a pair of smoking boots, the rest lost what little morale they had and ran off.

Ærin looked down at her sword and proclaimed, "I shall call you *Kettlingr.*" Then she turned to Magus. "Now what? I can't follow them in heavy armor, and we both know you'll get your ass kicked if you head on alone."

"Don't worry," said Petrov, "I can find them." He then walked over to the nearest hobo, picked said hobo up, slammed him into the wall, and shouted in his face "Vhere's Bromad? Vhat you know about him?"

"I don't know nuffen!" responded the hobo.

"A double negative!" roared Petrov, taking out his axe and shoving it in the hobo's face. "Vhere is he hiding?"

"He runs the adventurers' guild!" squealed the hobo, writhing in Petrov's grip. "The guildhall is up on Short Street!"

"Much better!" said Petrov. "Ve von't kill you. *Yet.*" Then he turned to the rest of the party and said "Bromad leads ze adventurers' guild, vhich is placed up on Short Street. Come on, let's go."

Ærin looked at him. "I'm all for fighting, but shouldn't we check the place out first? I mean, what if everyone in there is as powerful as we are?"

"Oh, fine. You humans and your caution," said Petrov. "Vhy, back in ze old country—"

"Nobody cares," said Magus. "Anyway, come on, let's check this building out."

******

The guildhall turned out to be a sturdy building of solid microcline. The windows had metal shutters that could be locked at a moments' notice, and the walls were coated in arrow slits and murder holes, making it obvious that no one would take it without a fight. Armed guards patrolled the rooftops and nearby alleyways at all times, supplemented by several people near the front trying so hard not to be seen that they were more conspicuous than if they were to stand out in the middle of the road. They weren't very good at guarding either, as it's not really that hard to notice a group of armed vigilantes standing on the sidewalk directly in front of your headquarters.

"There's no way we'll take that building without a fight," said Ærin, nicely recapping the situation for readers who skipped the previous paragraph. "We'll have to find another way in."

"How about the sewers?" said Magus. "We could head up through the—"

"No," responded Ærin.

"But—"

"No."

"Well then what should we do?" said Magus. "I suppose you could dress up as a whore and—"

"You know what," said Ærin. "If you think that's such a good idea, why don't you do it? You're the one wearing the dress."

"*Robe!*" shouted Magus. "It's a robe!"

"Same difference," said Ærin, right before flinging Magus through a window. "What's it like in there?"

"There's a lot of thugs," responded Magus. "I hate you—*Aghhhh!*"

Inside, Magus was surrounded and outnumbered twelve to one, and the leader of the thugs had just punched him in the gut. Magus fell to the floor.

"Staying down, little wizard?" said the thug. "We were hoping to have some fun first."

"No," said Magus, pushing himself up by his staff. "I am a wizard of the eighth arcane circle. I am a speaker at the council. I will still be alive while you are all moldering in your graves and you shall not talk to me that way! INFERNO ARDERE!"

Eldritch balefire burst from Magus's staff, burning with an eerie purple light. It flew toward the thugs, slamming into the one in the lead. The resulting explosion not only killed every one of the villains, it also shattered a huge hole in the wall and set the floor on fire.

Magus, standing alone unharmed in the middle of the flames, turned toward his companions looking directly at them with eyes that were now glowing an eldritch purple.

"Coming?"

******

Meanwhile, in the council room of the guildhall, all was not going well for Bromad. The guild had grown large, and all around him were people vying for his position. He was getting old and was starting to get tired of guild politics. Things just hadn't been the same ever since that raid on the nineteenth. The Empire had been cracking down, and the Emperor himself had made a statement saying that he disapproved of the smuggling, assassination, and other services the guild provided.

Suddenly the door to the counsel room burst open, interrupting Bromad's train of thought. Standing in the center of the doorway was a leather-clad kobold dual wielding punching daggers, a dwarf carrying a battleax and wearing purple robes emblazoned with spikes and hanging rings, and a Nordic-looking woman with red and orange armor, a red shield, and a sword with a green hilt. Oh yes, and some brown-haired freak wearing a blue dress. Probably a transvestite.

"Who are you?" shouted Bromad.

The freak in the dress stepped forward, pointed at Bromad, and said, "We are your death. EXTERMINARENT!" A fell green ray shot out of his upraised finger, and Bromad realized what the freak was far too late. *A wizard.*

******

All had been going according to plan. They had burst into the council room and Magus stepped forward and attempted to disintigrate the man in the center of the room—an aging fellow, with a military haircut and shifty blue eyes.

That was when things started going wrong. The green ray glanced off Bromad, who jumped up shouting, "I knew the magic armor was worth it!" before throwing off his cloak to reveal scale mail with runes inscribed on it in gold.

Bromad pulled out a sword before leaping at them, and Ærin had to jump back to avoid being skewered. Petrov rushed forward with his axe, but before he could reach them the rest of the people in the room recovered from their shock and drew their weapons as well.

Magus was in the middle of the fray, deflecting blows with his staff and trying to find an opening to use his dagger. His opponent, an ugly, wart-faced man, kept on the offensive, slashing in an X pattern that provided no openings. Magus backed away, but disaster struck when he tripped over a corpse.

The thug raised his sword above him, but suddenly fell forward. Magus looked up to see Petrov wrapping his arms around the guy, the spikes on his clothing penetrating wart-face's back.

"Get up manling! Ve've got vork to do."

Magus did so, but he stuck with Petrov, stabbing the dwarf's foes in the back when they were distracted. Eventually, the fight settled down until the only living enemy was Bromad, still fighting with Ærin. He attacked again, knocking Ærin's shield out of her hands. He pulled back for the killing blow, but found he could not. Ærin had pulled a hand-axe out of somewhere and used the hook at the bottom of the blade to grab his sword and pull it out of his grip.

As Ærin approached, raising her sword, Bromad's last thought was *Mommy.*

****

"Well that was easy," said Ærin. "Now for the hard part."

"The hard part?" said Magus. "I thought this was the hard part."

"Oh no," responded Ærin. "The hard part is where law enforcement chases us in an attempt to have us executed for being dangerously competent and contributing to the public order. Trust me, I know how this goes."

"This is the police!" shouted a voice from outside the guildhall. "Get on the floor and put your hands behind your head!"

"See what I mean?" said Ærin. "Come on, into the basement. We'll figure out what to do from there."

The basement was stone, entered by a steel door at the end of a long passage. Said passage was full of fortifications and arrow slits that couldn't be used from that side. This, along with the dwarvish lock on the door, made it obvious the basement was a panic room.

The bunker was filled with iron rations, weapons, and barrels of water. It was obvious Bromad had been planning to hold out in there for a long time. There was a patch of mud in one corner with huge and rather smelly purple mushrooms growing out of it, starkly contrasting with the rest of the room.

"Look!" shouted Petrov. "Plump helmets!"

"Plump helmets?" said Magus.

"Ve had zese back in old country!" replied Petrov. "I didn't know zat anyone grew zem here!" Petrov then sat down, plucked one of the mushrooms, and began eating it with every sign of enjoyment.

"Petrov?" said Magus. "Aren't you forgetting something?"

"Oh, yes," said Petrov. "I completely forgot about you guys. I'm sorry. Here you go." And with that, he threw each of them one of the vile fungi.

"No, Petrov," said Magus. "I meant the cops."

"I didn't forget about them," replied Petrov. "I just wanted a snack first." He got up, shoved the rest of the plump helmets into his pockets, looked over at the wall, and said, "This place ought to do." He then wacked the wall with the spike on the rear of his axe.

"Petrov?" said Magus, "What are you doing?"

"Mining our way out." replied Petrov. "Everyone and zeir mother have basement these days. If we mine through and brick up behind us, no one vill know!"

Petrov got into a steady rhythm, and soon they arrived in the wine cellar of some other building three blocks down. The place was cool and damp, with shelves and shelves of wine bottles stretching off into the distance. Petrov took a sip of the oldest one, spat it out, and said, "Foul human rubbish. I'll take vodka every time."

"Does it matter?" said Ærin. "Where are we?"

"Some rich guy's place," said Abda. "Only a nob would have a wine cellar this big. An army of dwarves would take fifty years to drink all this stuff."

"Why the *yebut* vould ve vant to?"

"Look," said Abda, "it vas a figure of speech!"

"Can we just get going?" asked Ærin. "If we stay here someone's bound to find us."

"And?" said Petrov.

"Well," said Magus, "the sane thing to do right now is leave."

"Sanity is for the veek!" shouted Petrov.

26

"Here, I'll make this simple," said Magus. "We leave this wine cellar or I kill everyone in it."

"Ha!" shouted Petrov. "Vizard boy, you couldn't hurt a fly."

"Really? ARDENS GAUDENDUM!"

As Magus spat out those words, a ball of flame burst out of his palm and hit a small casket of brandy, destroying the casket and scattering burning alcohol everywhere.

"Vhat the hell's wrong with you?" shouted Petrov.

"I'm sorry," said Magus, "I couldn't hear you over the sound of being surrounded by several thousand gallons of ethanol."

"Hey, vizard? Vhat say we go upstairs?"

"Much better."

So, they went upstairs, passing a fortune in dusty wine bottles as they did so. The upper half of the house exuded wealth, with mahogany floors and plaster-coated walls.

"Vhat a dump," said Petrov. "Vhy, back in the old country—"

"No one cares!" said Magus. "If the old country was so good, why did you choose to leave?"

"I fell out of favor with the Tzar."

"The who?" asked Abda.

"The Tzar—king. He and his nobles rule over our realm with an iron fist, squeezing money from peasants."

"This coming from someone who obviously used to be a peasant-squeezing noble," responded Magus.

"Vell, you see—"

Suddenly, a rough voice shouted, "Oy! Don't you know it's illegal to develop the plot in other people's homes! That's breaking and narrating, that is."

As the source of the voice came into view, the fellowship saw it was a guard wearing an imperial uniform. His face was—

"Hey! That goes for you too, mister. If you want to narrate, go do it somewhere else."

Did you just say what I think you just said?

"Yes, I did. Now get, out or we'll have you in chains."

Really... *Ahem:* **FOOLISH MORTAL! HOW DARE YOU ATTEMPT TO ARREST ME! I AM THE MASTER OF LIFE AND DEATH! I RULE ALL!**

As the guard stood dumbfounded like the insipid mortal fool he was, a bolt of purple lighting burst down from the ceiling and hit the guard right in the chest. His body flopped around in agony for several seconds as the eldritch flame burnt through muscle and sinew, until nothing was left but bones. Soon even these were consumed, leaving nothing but a gray powder.

As the heroes watched, somehow they knew that despite the fact that the guard's mortal form had been destroyed, his spirit was still alive in some nether-hell, soon to be eternally tormented by a foul demonic being that would leave him wracked in pain for what would be an unnaturally extended life.

"Wow," said Magus. "That was pretty well done. Next time maybe you could work on the insults a little though. Insipid seems a bit cliché. Be a bit more original next time. Maybe try something with maggots. Plus, the use of CapsLock is just overkill."

Thank you.

"Don't mention it. Anyway, can we get back on the road now?"

Oh all right, if you insist. The fellowship snuck onward. Nothing but the sound of their boots was heard. Well, the sounds of boots and armor. But the armor wasn't that loud. The sound was some sort of *Clang! Bang Crash! Bop-pting!* See? Not that loud at all.

"Hey!" said a guard, walking out of a darkened room. "Who are you? You can't be thieves, or at least not good ones. I could hear the sound of your armor from a mile away!"

Magus thought quickly. "Surprise inspection! Quick, where are you?"

"The baron's house," replied the guard.

"Good," said Magus. "Now, what are you supposed to do when you find a bunch of intruders dressed up as surprise inspectors?"

The guard thought for a bit and said "You're supposed to shout *'Guards, guards!'* and then—*argh!*"

That last bit there was not so much something he said voluntarily as much as it was something that you say when your internal organs have turned into kittens. Just in case you were wondering.

"Now what?" said Ærin. "We can't do that to all of them."

"Why not?" responded Petrov.

"Because, there'll be more people with them, and they'll probably notice the corpses," said Ærin.

"And? We're the heroes," said Petrov. "Winning when we're outnumbered ten to one is what we do."

"That sort of thing only happens in stories."

29

"Exactly!" said Petrov. "Look down there! A page number! This is a story."

"So was *The Horror at Insmouth,*" said Ærin. "That didn't have a happy ending."

Suddenly, a voice came out of the darkness! *Again!*

"Oy!" it said. "Wot the 'ell are you doing in 'ere?" Rather like the previous voice, this one belonged to a guard.

"Surprise inspection!" shouted Magus. "Quick, what you do when you find traitors disguised as surprise inspectors standing over the corpse of your comrade while contemplating how to kill you?"

"Well you're supposed to—*argh!*"

Turning back to Ærin after killing the guard Petrov smirked and said "Told you so."

******

"All right," said Ærin as they stood outside a large door labeled *Baron Von Dirigible's room. Keep out!* "This is the baron's room. Let's burst in and slaughter him."

"Why?" said Abda. "You guys may have grudges against the empire, but I don't."

You'll enter because I say so.

His mind suddenly changed, Abda followed Ærin as she bashed down the door. Inside, they saw a rug that probably had resulted in the genocide of some kind of small furry creature and a bed that could probably fit ten people although no one was really sure why it would need to. On the bed was a skinny man who probably thought of himself as rather dashing wearing nothing but a bathrobe. Beside him was a wizened kobold wearing lipstick. Both were in the process of taking their clothes off.

"*Aghhhh!*" shouted Magus, attempting to claw his eyes out. "*Brain bleach!* I need brain bleach!"

"It's not what it looks like!" shouted the baron. "And—wait, who are you?"

"Your death," said Ærin.

"Didn't we already use that line?" said Petrov.

"The death of *me*?" said the baron as he pulled a rapier out from under the bed. "I'm not just a rather dashing wizard; I'm also a good hand with a blade. I think you'll find that—"

There was a clatter as Ærin swatted the rapier from the baron's hand before he finished his dramatic monologue.

"Curse you, Rohirm fiend! A pox on you and your descendants! MAY YOUR CAR KEYS ALWAYS FALL INTO THE DEEPEST CREVICES OF THE SOFA, AND MAY YOUR SOCKS NEVER MATCH!"

"You call that a curse?" said Ærin when she finally stopped laughing.

"Well I'm new to this wizarding thing. Just skimmed the introduction packet, really. May I try again?"

"No."

"Crap."

******

"Now what?" asked Ærin.

"I think you used that line before, too," responded Petrov.

"*And?*" said Ærin. "We just killed the baron, the cops are after us, and I'm fairly certain we can't leave the same way we got in. What exactly do we plan on doing from here?"

"We know what *not* to do," said Magus. "For example, it's best we don't slit our throats to make the cops' lives easier."

"Thank you for that information."

Look, can you just stop arguing! I have a story to tell here!

"*And?*" shouted Magus. "There's no way out!"

Look, all you've got to do is... wait a minute; you're trying to get the solution from me, aren't you?

"Nonsense," said Magus. "We want a full-blown deus ex machina or nothing."

Like hell that's going to happen.

"Fine then. We're going to stay here and die, and this book will be rejected by every publisher who finds it. Your plots shall fade away into darkness and this shall become the greatest story never told."

Oh, all right. Look, the baron has an escape tunnel in the basement. Just get in there before anyone realizes he's dead and head on out.

"How convenient," said Magus. "Come on, let's go."

******

"I can't believe we didn't notice this the last time we were here," said Petrov. "I mean, it's got a glowing sign over it labeled *Escape Tunnel* and everything."

"It must have been hiding in hammerspace," responded Magus.

"Hammerspace?" asked Ærin.

"Highly complicated magical concept," responded Magus. "What it boils down to is that it's where the narrator keeps plot devices when they're not in use. It also functions as a portal to Chekov's armory. Anyway, let's head on in."

Magus and company walked on in, their footsteps echoing through the tunnel.

"Lousy human work," said Petrov. "Dwarf make would echo better."

"Why do you keep going on about how good the old country was if the place was so hard to live in?" shouted Magus.

"Things have changed since the elder days," responded Petrov. "One thousand years ago, back when I was a tiny beardling, our empire was at its height. The skies were filled with gyrocopters and airships, and the seas were tamed by our ironclads. However, we found a great treasure—one that would be our downfall. I had just one glimpse of adamantine during that time, and I have hoped for my entire life that I will get another. It was beautiful. It shined like silver, but with an azure luster. It had an inner strength that no blow could break, and although weapons made of it would never need to be sharpened, they had an edge that could cut through steel. Alas, it was our undoing. We tunneled down, down, determined to get more of this wonderful metal. Everything was perfect. We were winning the war with the elves, and the goblins had finally been cleansed from our lands."

"I had a job as a miner, and I was tunneling along the adamantine vein, when suddenly I discovered an eerie cavern. The air above the dark stone floor was alive with vortices of purple light and dark, boiling clouds. Seemingly bottomless glowing pits dotted the ground. Then, horrifying screams came from the darkness below! That was when I realized we had dug too greedily, and too deep, for—"

"You unleashed a shadow of fire and flame?" interrupted Magus.

"No," responded Petrov. "That was back in Sorok-D. This was worse. Down in the pit there were things. Eldritch things. Three-legged elephants with venomous spittle, vaporous beasts with noxious secretions, and flying, crystalline, dual-mouthed carp!"

"Carp," said Magus. "*Carp*. Do you really expect me to believe that you mined into Hell and found flying *carp*? And besides, if you mined into Hell, how are you still alive?"

"It wasn't much of a biggie," said Petrov. "Unlike you one-and-a-halflings, we weren't stuck in medieval stasis. Not even the fiends of Lodkaubity can survive being shot point-blank in the face."

"What, now you expect us to believe you conquered Hell?" said Ærin. "What kind of fools do you take us for?"

"But it really happened!" said Petrov. "We established a colony there and everything! That was not the event that destroyed the dwarven race, although that which did came soon after. You see, after colonizing hell, we did what any sensible dwarves would do. We held a party."

"And that was harmful why?" responded Magus.

"The dwarven race died," said Petrov. "Because that night... we didn't know when to say when."

"No, really!" he said, having apparently decided to forgo the accent. "The finest minds of our generation all died of acute liver failure that night. I thank Armok I was lucky enough to slip into a coma halfway through! Depopulated as they were, almost all the great dwarven holds fell to the elves that night! Glavapobegi, Strah Zimoĭ, Siroplista—all of them. In the end, we were reduced to huddling in the Mountainhome praying that they would go away. We have regained much of our land since then, but we are still spread thin, and we shall never regain our lost grandeur."

"I have a question," said Magus.

"What?" replied Petrov.

"Whatever happened to your accent?"

"Errr... vhat you mean?"

"Look, I just want you to stop screwing with us," said Magus. "Now tell me: what happened to the accent?"

"Nothing, comrade!" responded Petrov.

"Don't '*comrade*' me!" said Magus. "You just said the country is ruled by a Tzar. The fantasy equivalent of the Russian Revolution hasn't happened yet. Why all the Russian stereotypes?"

"*Vecause ve van!*" said Petrov.

"Look, just stop it, will you?" replied Magus. "There's no point! We already know you don't actually have an accent!"

"Vonsence!" said Petrov.

"Look," said Magus, "just tell us why you're using the accent."

"Look, do I have to have a reason? Can't I just adopt a fake accent for no reason at all?"

"No, not really."

"Fine then," said Petrov. "Let's just go on ahead. I think I see the exit. We're almost out!"

"It's a bit weird," said Magus. "You'd expect the baron to have been one of those load bearing bosses or something. Cause the entire place to fall down."

Thanks for reminding me. I almost forgot about the tunnel's self destruct sequence.

"FUUUUUUUUUUUUUU—"

******

"Now what?" said Ærin after the party had escaped the collapsing tunnel and emerged into a coniferous forest.

"Look, you've used that line almost four times," said Magus. "Try to be more original."

"It's still a valid question," said Ærin. "We're stuck outside a collapsed escape tunnel in a forest in the middle of nowhere and it's only a matter of time before the cops come after us."

"Simple. We have created a precedent. We killed the baron and there was nothing they could do about it. We shall rise up and tear the Empire stone from stone, starting with the baronies and ending with Ankhgard itself."

"Well that's nice and all," said Ærin, "but I meant in the short term."

"Look," said Magus. "I think I know where we are, and according to the map there's a town over there. Let's just head in and figure out what else to do tomorrow."

******

"'A town,' you said. 'Nearby,' you said."

"Shut up, Petrov," responded Magus. "This *is* a town."

"This isn't a *town*," said Petrov. "This is a group of thatched huts that huddle together for warmth."

As Magus looked around, he had to admit that Petrov was right. The largest building was the stone inn, a rather ramshackle affair whose ill cut stones only seemed to stay up via force of habit. All the other buildings were wattle and daub shacks housing the people who worked at the inn.

"Does it really matter?" Magus said. "There's going to be food and drink. What more do we need?"

"Hot water," said Abda.

"A roof that doesn't leak," said Ærin.

"A bed whose insects haven't yet discovered the wheel," said Petrov.

"Come on," whined Magus. "It can't be as bad as that."

******

Drip. Drip. Drip.

"We told you so."

"Look, I *said* I was sorry! Now will you just *shut up!*"

Drip. Drip. Drip.

******

"Out," said the innkeeper, rudely awakening them from sleep.

"Hey—" said Magus, but before he could finish, the innkeeper repeated, "*Out.* The empire's looking for you. I did you a favor by not turning you in the minute they knocked on my door."

"Look," said Magus. "Surely there must be something we can do to make you hide us."

"You don't understand the kind of trouble you're in, do you?" said the innkeeper. "They've sent a steam tank after you. *Out! Now!*"

Harried by the innkeeper's comments, the party ran out into the forest until they eventually reached a lake that barred all progress.

"All right," said Magus. "I think this is far enough. There's no way the Empire could have followed us to here."

"Dammit!" shouted Petrov. "You jinxed it!"

Then, there was a crashing sound. And another. And another. Suddenly, out of nowhere came a huge, boxy thing. It had two caterpillar threads on either side, with a central body that looked like a huge, mobile water tank. There were two slits in the front, each about the size of a human head, and a boxy thing on the top with a long nozzle protruding from it. In addition, there was an aperture on the back that belched smoke and steam. There were two arrow slits on either side of the central body, and positioned around it were ten imperial soldiers.

Six of the soldiers had standard gear with the exception of some metallic eggs pinned to their belts. Two in the rear of the party were carrying odd metal devices, and had several rods strapped to their back. One wore an odd mask made of leather and smoked glass, and carried some kind of apparatus attached by a hose to the metal barrel strapped onto his back.

As the soldiers moved, the nozzle attached to the device swiveled from side to side, and the formation changed so that none of the infantry were within its range, as if the device was about to spout some kind of horrible, flaming death. Then it turned toward the party and began to spout horrible, flaming death.

Said flaming death came in the form of what appeared to be liquid fire, which spouted from the machine in an arc. Ærin managed to block most of it with her shield, but quite a bit splattered beyond her and landed on the lake, where it continued to burn in defiance of all common sense.

"What the hell is that thing!" shouted Abda.

"It looks like some kind of tank!" responded Petrov. "The Imperials must have stolen the design!"

However, as quickly as the flame began to spout, it stopped, and from inside the tank came the sounds of cursing and someone hitting a pipe with a wrench.

Petrov took this as an opportunity to attack, shouting his battle cry of "Death to most tyrants!" as he leapt into a group of soldiers. The rest of the party tried to follow suit, but one of the masked soldiers bought his tube to bear, spraying flaming oil from its nozzle. Magus leaped over it, swinging his staff and denting the soldier's tube, but he suddenly realized he had left his party and was now right in the middle of a group of enemies, exactly the worst spot for a wizard to be.

He prepared for the inevitable beating, but it didn't come. When he looked up, he saw that the soldiers had all backed away, and one of the bombardiers was franticly shoving a rod into his device, while the other soldiers were kneeling and winding up the winches on their crossbows. Relieved, Magus waved a hand and a golden shield formed between them. Meanwhile, the tank had gotten the turret working again, but no matter what it did, the oil burst out over the heads of those nearby. Meanwhile, judging by the sounds coming from the other side of the machine, his comrades were doing just as well.

Then, unexpectedly, the rod burst from the bombardier's tube with a whoosh of flame, smashing through the golden barrier and heading right at Magus. He knew he had to act fast, so he quickly cast a spell.

"EST UT MI LABOS PERFLANT VENTIS. EST ICTU LABOS."

The gust of wind did not smash the missile into the ground as Magus had expected, but sent it right back at the soldiers. The formation simply stood still except for a soldier in the back who threw one of the eggs attached to his belt before the rod exploded, blowing him and his comrades to smithereens.

The egg missed Magus and fell to the ground nearby. He picked it up and looked at it. Then he remembered the tank. Magus leapt around and saw it had backed away, knocking his comrades over, and was now charging at him. He knew he had only seconds to live. In desperation, he threw the egg. It went straight through one of the vision slits in the front.

39

From inside the tank, he heard someone shout, and then there was an explosion. Bits of metal and odd pipework were thrown into the air, and burning oil was scattered about the landscape.

"*Dammit!*" shouted Magus. "Why does this kind of thing happen to me! Gandalf never had to deal with this steampunk crap! I mean, exploding metal eggs! What kind of insanity is this?"

"It was probably a *granat,*" replied Petrov. "Just in case being a dying race wasn't bad enough, we've got one-and-a-halflings all around trying to steal our technology. Why, back in the old county—"

"No one cares!" shouted Ærin. Then, after a moment of thought, she asked a logical question. "Now what?"

Chapter 3
Elf Qaeda

"Why so stereotyped?" said Magus.

"What do you mean?" said Abda. "This is my home. What did you expect it to be like?"

"Not like this!" Magus replied. "I mean look! Almost everyone's wearing a turban! Why, I wouldn't put it past this place to be ruled by a sultan!"

"Well, who else would you have ruling a country?" said Abda. "A king?"

"Of course!" said Magus.

"Look," said Abda. "It's our country and we have the right to live in a cliché. It's not like the Empire's any better. I mean aqueducts and fire engines? We might as well call them not-currently-ancient Grome!"

"Fine," responded Magus. "But we better not find any more Middle Eastern stereotypes, or else I leave, no matter what the danger in the Empire is. If I never see another minaret, it will be too soon."

"What about terrorists?"

"Terrorists, too! Blending time periods is almost as annoying as steampunk!"

"Then don't look in front of you."

Magus looked in front of him. As expected, insurgents were attacking one of the garrisons the empire had placed in the cities of its 'allies.' They were impressive, showing matrix-esque feats of agility, slaughtering the guards with ease. Soon, there was only one left: a kid just barely old enough to enlist, one that'd probably thought that he would get a medal by the end of the week. He was on his back in the dirt, attempting to scuttle away from the insurgents.

"Please!" he said. "Please don't kill me! I don't want to be here, I just got picked up by the draft! I've got a family, a life, and I can't go back to any of those if you kill me, pleasenonononononono," he said as he broke down and was reduced to incoherent babbling.

The insurgent at the head of the group, a tall man garbed head-to-toe in wrapped cloth simply reached down and broke the guard's neck.

Magus looked at the carnage in shock. Then, as the insurgents began to disperse into various alleyways he said "We have got to figure out how to join them."

"It's not that hard," said Abda. "This novel is rather linear. Here, watch," he said, gesturing to a hovel with smoke leaking from the holes in the roof. "I bet you that if we walked in there we'd find some kind of contact for them."

Inside the hovel were two fires, spaced equally within the confines. An old man in red robes stood between them. The floor was coated in so many layers of soot it was black as night, and the walls were a sickly green. The old man looked straight at Magus as if he could peer into his soul, before spreading his hands and saying, "Walk into the waterfall."

"Dammit," said Magus. "I have had it up to here with clichés. Tell us where to find the insurgents base or else."

"Walk into the waterfall," said the old man.

"Say that one more time and I kill you," said Magus.

"I know you won't hurt me," responded the old man. "So I say unto thee once again: Walk into the fucking waterfall!"

"…"

"*Argh!* My brittle, old man ribs!"

******

"Now what?" said Ærin. "Since idiot here killed the plot hook, there really isn't anything to do."

"Well," said Magus, "We could use this."

He pulled out a smallish book from a pocket that read, *The Hitchhiker's Guide to Elder Earth* on the spine and the words *Don't Panic* on the cover in large, friendly letters. "I found it in that dwarf's shop," he said by way of explanation.

"Nah," said Abda. "That thing will probably explode the first chance it gets."

"Come on," said Magus. "The dwarf was harmless. Well, mostly."

"Let's go," said Petrov. "We can just ask some random NPC[1] about the insurgents."

******

"'Ask a random NPC,' you said. 'It can't hurt,' you said."

"Well how was I supposed to know he was a cop?"

"He had a badge and a hat and everything!"

"I thought he was a cosplayer!"

Magus looked around at their surroundings, which were identical to those of their first prison, thus saving the need to describe it again. After a bit of thought, Magus said, "Why is it almost all of our adventures end with us in jail?"

---

[1] NPC is an offensive slur in the world of fiction, standing for Non Pertinent Character. It is used to refer to anyone the author is too lazy to name.

43

"Does it matter?" said Abda. "Anyway, I checked under the bed for the passage to the sewers, but it isn't here this time."

"Don't panic," said Magus. "I know how to escape. I'm a wizard; I can just fireball my way out."

"You idiot!" shouted Ærin. "Haven't you read the rulebook? This cell is just ten by ten! The blast would reflect back on us for twice the damage!"

"Besides," said Petrov, "Even if you could conceivably focus the blast well enough, we would be fried by convection long before it reached the melting point of rock."

"Will you shut up!" said Abda. "We're talking about science here!"

"We dwarves are the epitome of science! Why, back in the old country—"

"*No one cares!*"

"Anyway," said Ærin. "Now what? There's—"

Then, suddenly from the window, a voice rang out.

"I hear you're looking for the rebellion," it said.

"And what if we are?" responded Magus.

"First you must tell me," said the voice. "Friend or Foe."

"It depends," responded Magus. "What would you do if I said foe?"

"I have three barrels of black powder out here to cover your escape," replied the voice. "Don't make me move them any closer."

"Friend it is," said Magus. "I'm standing back."

****

"Why," panted Magus as he followed along behind the guide, "Did you have to build your secret base on the other end of a desert."

"If we put it in the middle of the city," said the guide, "it wouldn't stay a secret for long. We better stop now. Night is coming."

****

"Well," said Magus as he poked the fire with a stick, "I never expected to need a fire in the desert."

"Idiot," said Ærin. "What did you expect? Sand cools quickly."

"I know," said Magus, "but I didn't manage to put two and two together. Even with the fire, it's freezing cold. And what's with the noise? Why do all the creatures come out at night?"

"I will agree on that," said Ærin. "I haven't the faintest idea how the others manage to sleep through this."

"I suppose you get used to it after a while," said Magus. "You wouldn't believe what I got used to in my last gig."

"Actually," said Ærin, "I probably would, given that last year I discovered that lichen makes a really good pillow when you're tired enough."

"Yes," said Magus, "but was the lichen located in an H.P. Lovecraft novel? Mine was."

"Ouch," said Ærin, wincing.

"It wasn't actually that bad," continued Magus. "I was some kind of immortal wizard who fed off the life force of his ancestors, so I got to view the situation from the other side. Still, I wish I had snuck in a pillow or something. Sarcophagi are really uncomfortable."

45

"Idiot," said Ærin. "You know what the narrators do to any foreign objects people manage to sneak in."

"Why do you keep talking like that?" asked Magus. "It's not like you have to insult someone every other line."

"Actually," said Ærin, "I do. I'm a member of the Tsundere's guild. I presumed you would have realized that by now."

"Really?" said Magus. "I've never heard the term before."

"It's a portmanteau of a few foreign words for affection and disgust. That really sums the place up. Don't worry, I'm not on official business. Figured it would be best to play out of role, make sure I didn't get typecast."

"What's it like in there?" asked Magus.

"It's really nice. You get a guaranteed position in any Anime productions, and a cool looking membership card. Here, have a look."

Magus looked at the card, which had a rather nice picture of Ærin above a few eldritch sigils.

"Those?" said Ærin as she noticed him looking at the sigils. "They're the motto of the guild in its original language. They translate as—"

"Don't tell me," interrupted Magus. "I think I can translate it. I remember learning Kanji back when I was still an apprentice."

After a few seconds of Magus muttering things like "Bakka," and "Negative context," he looked up at Ærin and said, "Stupid Shinji? What kind of motto is that?"

"Ours," said Ærin. "Idiot. What did you expect? It's a quote from our founder."

"The Mage's guild never quotes our founder," said Magus. "Then again, it might have something to do with the fact that he was a cross-dresser."

******

"*Maaaaaguuuuusssss,*" moaned the spectral apparition as it materialized from the shadows. "I have a message for you from the world of the dead!"

Magus snored, as he had fallen asleep a few minutes ago.

"Wake up, idiot," said the ghost, crossing its arms. "I'm trying to deliver a prophecy here!"

"But Mommy," muttered Magus. "I don't wanna go to school-."

"Shut up," snapped the apparition. "Three problems. First: You've never met your parents. Second: If you had, you would not have gone to a school due to the lack of anything remotely resembling an education system. Third: That is the worst joke I have ever heard. It wasn't funny in whatever you stole it from, and it isn't funny now."

"Oh," said Magus, rolling over as he recognized the voice of Travia, his childhood ~~friend~~ ~~companion~~ acquaintance. "It's you."

Had Magus been drinking something when he saw Travia's blackened and scorched imperial armor and the third degree burns all over her face, he would have spat it out everywhere, and it would have been rather droll. Regrettably, supplies were being rationed, so he instead made a weird sputtering noise.

"The Emperor murdered me!" said Travia, apparently ignorant of the police report's contents. "I think he figured out that I was planning to betray him!"

"Yes," said Magus, putting on a poker face as he remembered the soldier he had killed in the prologue. "That is what happened. The Emperor truly is an awful person. Now then, about that prophecy?"

"Be patient!" snapped Travia. "I'm getting to it."

47

She cleared her throat.

"With elder staff and adamant sword
A lone hero goes to slay the Dark Lord.

As he walks through fire and flame,
He shall become the Tyrant's bane.

Aided by rogue, warrior, and midget
He really does look like an idiot."

"That last line didn't rhyme very well," said Magus. "You should see about getting a proofreader."

"I'm just not very good at rhyming," said Travia. "Perhaps I should work on my pacing."

"I give up."

****

"Behold! The waterfall!" shouted the guide.

"Look, will you stop practicing your dramatic reveal!" said Magus as the party walked through the trackless desert. "It's really getting annoying."

"Come on," whined the guide. "It isn't that bad!"

Suddenly, awakened by the annoying whining of a nameless side character, a giant desert scorpion unearthed itself from the sand.

"Told you so," said Magus.

"That was just a coincidi—*argh!*"

After impaling the guide on one of its claws, the vile beast turned his attention to Magus, who promptly ran and hid behind a rock.

"That was brave of you," said Ærin.

48

"Honor is for suckers," said Magus. "Besides, *you're* one to talk. You're hiding here too!"

"I'm not hiding; I retreated in order to loop around and flank the enemy."

"You're hiding."

"Bah," said Ærin, looking from side to side. "Where's Petrov?"

"*Death to most tyrants!*"

"Crap."

As Magus turned, he saw Petrov leaping out at the scorpion while spewing an impressive amount of profanity.

"Dammit, Petrov!" shouted Magus. "Get away from that thing! You'll get yourself killed!"

"The bigger they come, the harder they fall!" Petrov called back as he dodged a swipe of the scorpion's tail.

"If that thing falls it'll land on you!" Magus shouted quickly, hoping not to draw the beast's ire his way.

"All trees are felled at ground height!" said Petrov.

"Some trees are not meant to be felled!" responded Magus.

"Look, will you just help?" shouted Petrov.

"He's right, you know," said Abda. "We can't sneak past that thing and we're going to need the guide's map if we want to get out."

"Very well," said Magus, raising his staff high in the air. "For death! For honor! For glory!"

With those words, the party rose from behind the rock and attacked.

Well, most of it at any rate.

"Look," said Magus. "I'm the mage! Never mind the giant scorpion; I would probably die if someone *looked* at me too hard!"

Bah! It's just a giant desert scorpion. The worst it can do is poison you, grab your staff and then beat you to death with it.

"Why does that fail to reassure me? Anyway, how does the scorpion work?"

What do you mean, work? It has blood and stuff, just like everything else.

"Yes," said Magus, "but what about the square-cube law?"

Huh?

"When you square the size of something, you cube the stress on its material components. That scorpion's legs should snap, and if they were large enough to hold it up, it wouldn't be able to get enough oxygen to fuel the muscles."

Are you sure?

"Yes."

Fine.

Elated at catching one of its few repeat offenders, whatever enforces the laws of physics came down on the giant desert scorpion like a ton of bricks, mashing it to a pulp. Magus simply watched and smirked like the moronic asshole he was, knowing fully well he had ruined the suspense, and that there would now be no chance for the narrator to use something cool like a dragon, as he had gone and found a cheap way to kill anything that wasn't completely mundane. Bastard.

"Congratulations!" said the idiot. "You just managed to become more biased then Fox News."

"Can you just leave the fourth wall alone?" said Petrov. "We've got the map, so let's get going."

******

"Behold!" shouted Petrov. "The waterfall!"

"Hooray," said Magus. "A waterfall. Can we enter now?"

"Fine."

As Magus entered, walking straight through the misty spray, he saw a flicker of movement out of the corner of his eye, but it was probably nothing. Then, everything went black.

******

Magus woke up. His eyes opened, and they flitted around, quickly taking in the surroundings. Not much to look, at really. A black room, the black chair he was sitting in, the torch shining into his eyes, that kind of thing. He tried to get up and discovered he was tied to the chair. Oh, and did I mention the ominous figures standing around the room? There were a lot of ominous figures standing around the room, each with black cloth wrapped around their heads as improvised masks that obscured all but their eyes.

"Tell me," said the figure in the front, obviously the leader. "Why were you looking for our base?"

"We were looking for the insurgents," said Magus. "We wanted to join."

"Hrmmm..." muttered the leader. Then, Magus suddenly felt an odd presence feeling about in his mind. He tried to resist, but he could halt it no more than the Pillsbury Dough Boy could stop a steamroller.

After a few seconds, the presence retreated, and the leader said, "He is telling the truth."

He then snapped his fingers, and the bonds trapping Magus sprung off and set him free.

"Who are you?" said Magus as he was getting up. "And why do you all have towels wrapped around your heads?"

"Because we couldn't find anyone who sold ski masks in bulk... and as to who we are... We are the insurgents. And I.... am Aragon Ælfhame."

As he said this, the man took off his towel, revealing features that would have been totally unremarkable if you did not notice the soulless cat-like eyes, and the eerie, inhuman face.

When he saw the man and heard his name, Magus gasped, because he had been hearing tales of him his entire childhood. While some myths said he had sold his soul to the fey folk, while others said he had joined the elves to fight the Empire, no two stories were even remotely alike.

"Come on," said Aragon. "Your friends are waiting and there's good that needs doing."

******

"How is blowing up a school doing good?" asked Magus as they lurked outside a one-room schoolhouse.

"It's for the *greater* good," responded Aragon.

"Ah," said Magus. "This is obviously some form of the word good of which I was previously unaware."

"What did you just say?" asked Aragon with a tone of menace that made it obvious he had heard exactly what Magus said.

"I said 'yes sir,'" replied Magus.

"Very good."

******

"All right," shouted Aragon as he kicked down the schoolhouse door. "Don't nobody move!"

"Wait," said the teacher, a balding man with blue eyes and glasses. "Do you mean that we *should* move? That's a double negative, you know."

"You moved!" Aragon shouted as he conjured up a blast of eldritch flame, instantly incinerating the old man. "Now then Magus," he said while pointing at a crying red haired kid of ambiguous gender, "kill that kid."

"But... she's a kid!" said Magus.

"And?" responded Aragon. "She moved."

"No," said Magus. "It's wrong. I may not be much of a hero but I have to stand up against something."

"You know," said Aragon, ignoring Magus's previous comment. "There was a butcher I knew once. Out of fear, in an attempt to save his family, he betrayed my brother. For that, he lost his eyes. But you know what? That wasn't enough. By the time I was done with him, he had lost everything. His friends, his home, his family, and his way of life. I left him in the middle of the desert, eternally starving yet unable to die, until the geas I put on him drew him into the tender mercy of the elves. Are you sure you want to risk that?"

"Not only shall he risk it," said Petrov, "But I shall risk it at his side. Magus, you have my axe."

"And my sword," said Ærin.

"And my dagger," said Abda.

Magus looked up at Aragon and said "Your move."

"Very well." Suddenly, Aragon jumped, arcing over them in a leap that would have been really dramatic if it wasn't for the really low celling in that building. As it was, he hit his head on a rafter and knocked himself out.

"That was anticlimactic," said Magus.

Then, inside his head came a thought that was not his own. The foreign voice screeched, resonating with power as it shouted *"Good, for the worst is yet to come!"*

Wood creaked and snapped as the roof was ripped off and flung aside by some creature larger than a house, with claws like knives and breath like a jet engine. Its scaly, reptilian hide was a midnight blue, and its eyes glowed as red as the fires of hell.

"A dragon?" said Magus. "Really? After what we did to the scorpion a few pages ago? ANTIMAGIC-"

"No," said the voice, behind which ran an intelligence so ancient and powerful that it almost destroyed Magus's mind on the spot. This was a creature so outlandish, so alien to normal human thought, that being connected to it would by all rights drive a man mad.

"Look, will you stop that? You may be the narrator, but that doesn't mean you can describe how I'm feeling. Last gig I got was in a story written by a Lovecraft fan, so unless you have a blasphemous abomination with eight ever-screaming mouths wailing from the ceaseless agony of existence while devouring its enemies whole and digesting them as they still live, there's no way you're going to scare me."

54

Hey, that's actually a very good idea.

"Great," said Ærin. "You're giving him ideas. Please shut up now."

"You do realize that I'm still here, right?"

"Hush now," said Magus. "The grownups are talking."

"I shall hush when you are in your graves!" said the dragon as its mouth opened, revealing the glowing pilot light deep behind its uvula.

"Look," said Magus, "You can't flame us. You'll kill Aragon, too."

"Hrmmm..." muttered the dragon. Then, it lowered its claw onto Magus, pinning him to the ground so that it would only have to move an inch in order to decapitate him. *"You have a point,"* it said.

"May I have some last words?" said Magus.

"Very well," the dragon murmured. *"But make it quick."*

"Potestatem habeo de Deus Ex Machina!" shouted Magus, before both he and his comrades disappeared with a flash of purple light.

"How the hell did they get away?" thought the dragon.

A wizard did it, Aragon thought back.

Chapter 4
Khazad-Dumb

"Are we all in agweement? If any think otherwise, speak up now."

"We are all in agreement."

"Vewy well, Ioseb. The Plan is to continue unaltered. This meeting of the people's Fifth Soviet is concwuded. And didn't happen."

******

Magus looked around. The room he was in looked like none he had ever seen before. The walls were of solid microcline, not piled up in blocks but carved out of the living stone. He did not know why the spell had brought him to this place, nor how he managed to avoid teleporting into the rock wall itself, but he knew it was probably important.

"We are all going to die," said Petrov. "I have seen this place before."

"Come on," said Magus. "It can't be as bad as that."

"It can," replied Petrov. "For we are now guests of the Tzar."

******

"Who are you?" the Tzar boomed as Magus was herded into the room by a squad of armed guards. "And why do you trespass in my domain?"

"O great and noble Tzar," said Magus, looking up at the bearded, purple-clad figure sitting before him on a golden throne. "We were simply—"

"*Silence!* Your trial shall begin immediately."

Magus sighed. It was going to be a very long day.

******

"So," intoned the Tzar, taking a small piece of paper from the jurors, "The verdict is... *not* guilty?"

His face scrunched up, and he waved to the guards, who herded the jury from the room. After a few minutes the guards returned alone, coated in bloodstains.

"So," intoned the Tzar, taking a small piece of paper from the ~~guards~~ replacement jurors, "The verdict is... *Guilty*. A wise choice. I sentence you to fifty years in the labor camps, to slave until your arms drop off. Guards, away with them."

As the guards dragged Magus and his comrades away, the Tzar smiled. It was going to be a very good day.

******

"Now what?" said Petrov.

"Hey!" said Ærin. "That's *my* catchphrase! Don't make me sue you!"

"And why can't I use it?" argued Petrov. "I had the good fortune to be exiled, and I was free for the last fifty years before you idiots got me into this!"

"And?" said Magus. "I'll get us out."

"How?" responded Petrov. "The gulag might as well be an oubliette! I should know! I designed this place myself!"

As Magus looked around, he had to admit Petrov was right. They were at the bottom of a huge quarry, its stone walls towering far above them. Hundreds of dwarves labored alongside them, some digging up marble, others smoothing it into cubes for construction use. Three times each day, food was dropped through a system of chutes, and although there were no observable exits, somehow each night, the marble blocks they had made by day were removed. There were—

57

"Wait!" said Magus. "That's it! We can just hide ourselves in the block pile and-"

"No," said Petrov. "We can't. The blocks are checked by guards before being loaded onto a train that winds through thirty miles of tunnels. Even if we could sneak out we'd end up starving to death. Furthermore, engraved in the walls every five miles are runes that suppress any kind of magic, and even if they weren't there, those bracers you're wearing should stop you from doing anything more than pulling Ping-Pong balls out of peoples' ears. Our weapons are gone, our armor is gone, and our freedom is gone. There is no way out."

"There's always a way out," responded Magus.

"That there is," said another dwarf, who seemed to have appeared out of nowhere. He wore a grey business suit, and oddly enough, had no beard.

Petrov gaped in shock. "What have they done to you?"

"Nothing... but that does not... matter?" responded the dwarf, slurring through some words and pausing at random points as if he was not used to the language.[2] "The runes will be dessstroyed later this... month. Be prepared."

"Are you sure you can do it?" said Magus. "No offence, but a mysterious figure from nowhere helping us for no apparent reason sounds slightly less than reliable."

"Of course I can," the dwarf declared.

"Very well," said Magus. "One more thing: What's your name?"

"It mattersss not," responded the dwarf. "I ssshall contact you again... soon?"

******

---

[2] Or as if he was drunk. Your call really.

It was several weeks before they heard from the mysterious figure again, by which point the dismal food and damp floors had almost driven them mad. They had remained secluded from the other inmates for the entire time, lest they turn on them if the escape attempt failed. Finally, he appeared, simply walking out of the crowd while the prisoners were having the daily brawl over who got first pick of the food. He looked straight at Magus with eyes of endless night before saying naught but one word.

"Tomorrow."

"Wait," said Magus, but it was too late, for the figure had already dissolved back into the crowd.

"Bastard," said Petrov vaguely. "Almost as bad as the G-Man."

"Look," said Magus. "Would you mind keeping the fourth wall at least vaguely intact? There's no way you would be able to know about him."

"I had all four of the Half Life games at one point," responded Petrov. "How could I not know about him?"[3]

"How could you have played them?" asked Magus. "No offence, but I highly doubt that you have an Xbox."

"Well of course," said Petrov. "How would I manage to get my hands on one of those?"

"Then how—" said Magus, but Petrov quickly cut him off.

"I had a PC," he said.

******

"Now," said Magus, his eyes flashing gold for a second, illuminating the darkened quarry.

---

[3] It's been fifteen thousand years and they still haven't released Episode Three.

"How do you know?" asked Abda.

"Magic," responded Magus.

"You get some kind of thrill out of being annoyingly cryptic, don't you?" said Abda.

"I'd make a comment about it being crack for wizards," replied Magus, "but I'm pretty sure the Dresden files already did that one."

"Weren't you the one complaining about the fourth wall being broken?" responded Abda.

"Yes," said Magus, "but it's okay when I do it because... because... because I say so."

"Does it matter?" said Petrov. "Even with the runes destroyed, you still have those bracers on."

"Yes, but I still have *this!*" said Magus triumphantly as he reached far deeper into his pocket than the garment should have been able to allow and slowly pulled out his staff.

"'Is that an engraved quarterstaff in your pocket," said Ærin, "or are you just happy to see me?"

"Both, actually," said Magus, "But that's not important right now. With my staff, I can focus the magic enough to overpower the bracers! Here, watch!"

He reached toward Petrov and said,

"An nota nihil manica meam."

As he spoke, his hands began to tremble, and the chunk of quartz at the top of his staff began to glow. As he tightened his control over the ether more and more, a vein in Magus's forehead began to pulsate and his staff began to smoke. Everyone thought he might kill himself with the strain when suddenly he reached forward and gave a sigh of relief as he pulled a Ping-Pong ball out of Petrov's ear.

"Is that it!" cried Petrov. "You plan to break us out of the gulag with a Ping-Pong ball! I might as well slit my own throat and save the guards the trouble!"

"No," said Magus, "That was just an example. I plan to break us out like this: MI CEREBRUM CLAVIS EST ANIMUS FACIT LIBERUM."

Suddenly, the locks on his bracers flicked off and fell aside. Almost simultaneously, the glowing runes, engraved a full thirty feet up on the wall exploded. As their glow faded and the chunks of rock began to fall, Magus's eyes began to glow an eerie purple, and his staff shone an iridescent blue.

"Let us go," he said, "There is much work to do." Several explosions blasted from far off, and the sounds of steel on bone began to emanate from the darkness.

"Well, wizard boy?" asked Petrov. "How do you plan to get us out of this one?"

"Well," said Magus, "do you remember what I said back in chapter two?"

"You mean—" said Petrov but Magus quickly cut him off.

"Yes. Let us go. "

******

"Are you ready, wizard boy?" said Petrov.

"As I'll ever be," responded Magus. "QUI CONCIDENT GLADIOS SUOS IN VOMERES OPERANTUR ERIT HIS QUI NON!"

Instantly, two bursts of energy flew down from the shadowed roof, impacting the ground parallel to each other in front of Magus's feet. As the lights grew ever brighter, the space between the bolts began to writhe and struggle, as if the very fabric of time and space was in the process of being ironed. Soon, the wriggling filaments began to wind together and intertwine, and slowly formed an oval, perfectly shaped and seemingly without human error.

It shined a vivid blue light, and radiated glowing tendrils of a coruscating violet so dark as to seem almost black. As the spell began to approach critical mass, a vein in Magus's forehead began to pulse, and the crystal on the tip of his staff began to glow red and smoke. Then, Magus gave a sigh of relief and the tendrils recessed into a border, surrounding the hole in space. Through it, another realm could be seen, one with stone floors, roof and walls. There were metal hooks coming out of the walls in several places, each with some kind of weapon hung from them.

"Is that all!" said Petrov. "It was nothing but lights and the effect on you was borrowed from last time!"

"I just opened a portal into another universe!" responded Magus. "What did you expect other than lights? Let's go."

****

"That was rather anticlimactic for dimensional travel," said Abda as they came back out of the portal and returned to reality. "I expected there'd be monsters or something in there."

"Look," said Magus. "Can we get back on track? We've got weapons now, and there's a lot of killing that needs to be done."

"You still haven't gotten us out yet."

"Really?" asked Magus. "SCIS, SUUS VERE DIFFICILIA NOMINA CUM LEPIDUS OMNIUM CARMINIBUS!" Then he raised a finger, pointed at the wall and said, "SUM TETENDIT!"

As he said those words, a ten-foot-by-ten-foot portion of the wall suddenly disappeared, leaving nothing but a wisp of smoke to mark its disappearance. The resulting tunnel continued until it hit another tunnel exactly one hundred feet away.

"Wait," said Abda. "You teleported us in the last chapter. Why can't you do that again? It could solve all our problems. We just teleport into the Emperor's throne room, kill him, and get out before anyone notices."

"Teleporting isn't an exact science," said Magus. "I managed it before, but this time we might appear in solid rock, or leave our skeletons behind. I'm not sure about you guys, but I'm rather attached to my skeleton, so teleporting is reserved for when there's no other option."

Can you get along with the story now?

"Fine."

The fellowship rushed through the tunnels, but as they ran they soon became lost in the maze of twisted passages. Suddenly, darkness fell like a drunken man stumbling along the edge of a cliff. It was now very dark. They were likely to be eaten by a grue.

"All right," shouted Magus. "Enough of this mystery crap! What the hell is a grue?"

The thing that's right behind you!

"Not funny."

Fine. The lights go back on. Happy now?

"Yes," said Magus as the lights went back on.

"Why did you have to antagonize him like that?" said Petrov.

"Because it's what I do," responded Magus. "Besides, why do you care?"

"Because," said Petrov. "There are *things* in the deep... Foul beasts that have no name. Antagonizing the narrator is sure to draw their ire. Listen! The trumpeting! It comes! *It comes!*"

As Magus listened, he could hear muffled trumpeting, like Godzilla with a clogged nostril, and then suddenly a pale, eyeless elephant with external ribs emerged from the darkness. Its tusks were long and gleaming, and it appeared emaciated.

"The Spawn of Atu has come!" exclaimed Petrov. "Beware its deadly dust!"

As soon as Petrov uttered those words, the monstrosity sucked in air and then released a writhing, billowing cloud from the holes in its chest. Petrov jumped to avoid the dust, but the billowing cloud enveloped him, rolling over his head and obscuring him from view.

"Flee!" shouted Magus. "I'll hold it off! A STETTIN BALTIC UT IN TRIESTE IN ADRATIC, FERREA CORTINA HABET DESCENDIT IN CONTINENTI!"

Suddenly a blue translucent wall appeared between Magus and the monster, cutting off the gas and separating them from the enemy.

"Don't worry about me!" shouted Magus. "I'll slow it down!"

"All right," said Petrov as he got up and staggered off with Ærin and Abda following behind.

"Wait!" shouted Magus. "No! You're supposed to try to talk me out of it! Wait for me oh gods it's breaking through get it off get it off get it off argh!"

****

"You know," said Abda, "We really ought to have a moment of silence for Magus. He gave up his life for us."

There was a brief moment of silence as they sat around the pile of burning fungus, hiding in its glow from the shadows of the cavern and that which lived within.

"All right, moment over," said Ærin.

"I know it's not much, but I think we should say something," responded Abda. "After all, *he* would, if it were one of us who had died."

After a moment's thought, Ærin looked up and proclaimed "Better him than us. Besides, we have more important things to worry about."

"Like what?" said Abda.

"Like that dust," responded Ærin. "Petrov, are you all right?"

"Don't worry," said Petrov. "I was feeling drowsy for a bit there, but now I'm fine. That's the weird thing about beast sickness. Sometimes it'll make you bleed so fast your blood might as well be teleporting outside your body, and sometimes it'll just make you walk funny and avoid fruit."

"Well, I'm glad that's covered, then," said Abda. "Now then, what do we have to eat?'

****

"I told you foraging was a bad idea," said Ærin as they walked through the cavern, glancing about in the circle of light that their torch provided. "Now we're hungry and lost."

"Yes, but we were hungry and lost before this too," responded Abda. "Besides, we're bound to come across something eventually."

"Hey, guys!" shouted Petrov from off in the darkness. "Come see what I found!"

As Ærin and Abda approached Petrov, they noticed a huge, rectangular building, made out of some kind of smooth grey stone that towered above all else in the cavern. Petrov was in front of it, closely examining some type of fungal bush.

"By the Allfather's eye!" exclaimed Ærin. "What kind of wizardry is this?"

"What kind of wizardry is what?" said Petrov, turning. "*Bozhe moǐ!*" He said when after looking up. "I didn't notice that before. I actually called you over here because I'm pretty sure we can eat that bush."

"How sure is *pretty sure?*" asked Ærin.

"There's only a fifty to one chance of you dying painfully," responded Petrov.

"That's pretty safe," said Abda. "I wouldn't bet on a horse with those odds."

"Look," said Ærin. "Let's just head in there. Whoever lives in that tower is bound to have food."

****

"'Head in there,' you said. 'Bound to have food,' you said."

"Shut up Petrov," responded Ærin. "How was I supposed to know the place was filled with zombies?"

"You should have *assumed* it was full of zombies!" exclaimed Petrov. "Besides, why are we even trying to fight through them? The way out is over there!"

"Because," said Ærin, "any adventurer worth their salt knows that all places abandoned by their original owners and colonized by monsters are going to inexplicably have a lot of treasure in the center."

"Inexplicably, my ass," responded Petrov. "The stuff probably belonged to all the other idiots who thought the same thing."

"Look, will you both shut up!" said Abda. "We're nearing the center, and we'll have to sneak in if we want to surprise the boss monster."

"Fine," grumbled Petrov. "But don't think I've forgotten this."

"Look, will you just be quiet?" said Ærin. "The boss monster might notice us!"

Suddenly, each and every one of them felt something. A word... A presence... They were not sure, but it had a voice of unimaginable menace, and the voice spoke naught but three words:

I SEE YOU!

Then, intangible threads began to wrap around them, lifting them up and slamming them into the wall. Through the supernaturally induced pain, they saw a huge creature float up from the stairwell in the center of the room. The beast had a vaguely cylindrical body and yellow eyes with eerie, curving pupils. There were eight shapeless appendages dangling around its beak, and two spiked tentacles extending from either side.

"Oh come on," said Petrov. "A psychic cuttlefish?"

It's not a cuttlefish! It's an Aggregate Advisor!

"It's a psychic cuttlefish."

Cuttlefish or not the thing will still be powerful enough to kill you.

"We are the heroes. Nothing will stop us."

I'm the narrator. I get to make things stop you.

"Really?" said a voice. "SAEPIA PEDICABO!"

A beam of light burst from the darkness in the back of the room, ramming into the cuttlefish and knocking it to the ground, as well as illuminating the darkened corner and revealing what appeared to be a man wearing a dress.

"Magus?" said Abda, unable to believe his eyes.

"The very same," said Magus. "But right now I believe we have more important things to worry about."

Even as Magus said those words, the cuttlefish regained its balance and swooped at him screeching, *YOU SHALL NOT TAKE THE SWORD!*

"Yes, I shall," said Magus. "It's over. Surrender."

SURRENDER! PITIFUL FOOL! I AM STRONG WHILE YOU ARE WEAK. YOU ARE BUT CHILDREN WHEREAS I AM AGELESS. I NEED NOT SURRENDER TO THE LIKES OF YOU.

"Then you shall die. SUM LASERS PRÆCIPIENS!"

WHAT IS THIS I DON'T EVEN—

****

"There we go," said Magus once the cuttlefish had been reduced to ash. "Problem solved."

"But how did you manage to survive?" asked Petrov.

"I almost didn't," responded Magus. "I fought the beast, chasing it from cavern to cavern, and from the bottom of the Endless Staircase to the very top. There I slayed my enemy, and he smote the mountainside in his fall."

"Wait a minute," said Ærin. "Are you trying to convince us that the Endless Staircase has a top and a bottom?"

"Are you calling me a liar?" responded Magus.

"Yes, I am," said Ærin.

"Good." responded Magus. "I was afraid you were setting up some kind of horrible Tolkien pun."

"What kind of girl do you think I am?"

"The sort that makes bad Tolkien puns," responded Magus. "Now then, where was I? Ah yes... After I had slain my foe, I felt a rush of power. I had changed. I had evolved. Now, I am Magus the Blue!"

"I thought you were already Magus the Blue," said Abda.

"Sort of," responded Magus. "You see, when a wizard finishes his apprenticeship or does some amazing feat of magic, he gets to choose his color, but until then he has to put up with the one his master gave him, and since mine died, I was stuck with what he gave me."

"Well then, what were you before?" asked Petrov.

"I was Magus The Sort Of Violetish Turquoise."

"No, really!" he said when his companions had finished laughing. "Anyway, there are more important things to worry about. For starters, what was the monster talking about?"

"Well," said Ærin. "It might have something to do with the room below us that probably contains lots of treasure and can only be entered via the stairwell that thing was guarding. What do you think?"

"Either way," said Magus, "I suppose we'll have to check."

****

The room was large, taking up the entire floor. In the exact center, there was a blue sword embedded in a translucent pedestal.

69

"It's mine," said Magus. As he drew nearer to the sword, he began to hear a faint humming, as if it was gently vibrating. The blade was undecorated, and the hilt was plain, but it appeared highly impressive, and looked sharp enough to cut the air.

"Really bad craftsmanship," said Petrov. "Dwarf make would hum better."

"Oh, shut up," responded Magus as he drew the sword from the pedestal. As soon as he did so, the humming ceased, and the pedestal vanished into thin air.

"You shouldn't have done that," said the sword. "Look down."

Magus looked down into the newly uncovered abyss, and the abyss stared right back.

"Motherfu—"

Chapter 5
Orpheus can suck my Gonarch

"—cker!" shouted Magus. Looking down, he saw a spiral staircase of dark grey stone looping down to a dark abyss made up of a dark grey stone, lit with eerie purple light. At the bottom there were innumerable abominations, each one seemingly made out of the bits the gods had left over. All were coated with eyeballs and mandibles, and none were even remotely alike. There were wraiths of steam, tentacle brutes, grime banishes and wraiths of flame, all charging. However, even a horde as diverse as this has one thing in common. In this case, they were all charging the wrong way.

"Are those things running away from us?' asked Ærin.

"Nonsense," said the sword. "They're all running at something."

"Shut up," said Magus. "Swords can't talk. They'd need lungs and things."

"What, like vocal cords?" asked the sword.

"Yeah," said Magus, "That kind of stuff."

"Look," said Abda. "It's obvious we're supposed to head down there, so let's just get to it."

****

"Remind me," said Magus, "Why was this considered a good idea?"

"I really wish I knew," responded Abda.

Look, it's just a betentacled purple thing that oozes noxious secretions! Just attack already so we can move the plot along!

"No way we're attacking that thing!" shouted the sword. "I refuse to touch it. Someone else can fight that."

"That's a great idea," said Magus. "Ærin, why you go fight it?"

"Like hell I will," said Ærin. "I know a genre change when I see it. That thing gets within five feet of me and there'll be a lawsuit before you freaks can say sexual harassment."

Look, it's not like that! It was a Lovecraft reference!

"That's what they always say. Pervert."

The tentacle monster burbled.

"And why don't you just shut the fuck up!"

Ærin's thrown sword pierced the monster, chopping off one its tentacles and causing a noise like someone poking a hole in the world's largest balloon. Huge amounts of glistening fluid sprayed from the hole as the creature fell to the ground and slowly flattened.

"Damn new sword," said Ærin. "The balance is all wrong. I swear, the Tzar will be the first to die when I get Kettlingr back."

"Look, can we at least get to work on something?" said Magus. "For starters, where are all the monsters heading?"

"I think they're rushing at that grey thing in the distance," said the sword. "Why don't we go see what it is?"

"Shut up," said Magus. "Swords can't talk. Anyway, anything the demons want to get closer to is probably best left alone. I vote running from it."

"Yes," said Petrov. "Why don't we walk across this infinite hellscape with no end in sight and eventually die of starvation? The grey thing is the only landmark in sight. We can either head for it or slit our throats here and now."

"No!" shouted Magus. "We are not going anywhere near that thing. For all we know, it's some vile beast that the demons all worship or something. I refuse. We are not going anywhere near that thing!"

****

Surprisingly enough, the greyish object turned out to be a huge, cyclopean fortress and not a dark god at all. The demons were charging at it and being mowed down by hidden machine gun nests. The smooth microcline blocks fit together perfectly, and it was obviously built to last.

"Well," said Magus. "That's nice and all, but how are we going to get inside?"

"Magic," said Abda.

"Gee, that's useful," snarked Magus. "'*Magic.*' You might as well say we get nutrition by eating. There's no other way in. What I want to know is how we're supposed to use it."

"What do you mean use?" responded Abda. "I thought you just wave your hands to make stuff happen."

"Yeah, it doesn't work like that," responded Magus. "If I wanted to create a spell of darkness, then I'd have to figure out which fluctuations in the ambient gasses will interact in the greater chthonic matrix in order to defect light waves in a certain area, and that's without even defining the location and duration of the spell. For that, I'd need to-"

"Yeah, I get the point," said Abda. "Magic is harder than we think. Can you shut up now?"

"No."

As they bickered, the rush of demons at the fortress slowed down suddenly, until the torrent became a trickle.

"Wow," said Magus.

"Yes," responded a voice. "Wow."

After a momentary pause, Magus felt metal at his back. "Now then," said the voice, "Turn around or I gut you."

As Magus turned, he saw three dwarves: two were steel-clad and wielded bolt action rifles, while one wore plate-mail composed of a blue, silvery metal and carried a battle axe made of the same material. The axe looked sharp enough to cut through a concrete block, and certainly sharp enough to cut through a ~~crossdressing murderhobo~~ wizard.

Despite the obvious primitiveness of his choice of weapon compared to the others, for some reason the dwarf wielding it managed to project an aura of power that made him appear far more dangerous than anyone else in his presence.

"Who are you?" asked Magus.

"I am Commander Kozhi, leader of the military of Smertnyhdrozhat' and Dubinoïroman," replied the dwarf in the lead. "You appear to be the man who burst into the Tzar's palace and recently escaped into the caverns. Now then, we can do this the easy way, or the easier way."

"What's the easy way?" asked Magus.

"You come with us," responded Kozhi.

"And the easier way?"

"I gut you and leave you for the demons."

"The easy way it is."

****

"You idiot!" shouted Ærin as the guards shoved the party into a prison cell before shutting the door with a clang. "If you had just attacked, that weapon you had would have cut through their armor like a hot knife through butter. Instead, you've gotten us captured again, and we'll soon be right back where we started."

"Byk!" spat Petrov. "That was adamantine that dwarf was wearing. If we attacked, we would have been slaughtered. That stuff can cut through steel as if it was paper, and through rope reed fiber as if it were air. We would have been dead, and if we try something we will die. There is no escape. We are doomed."

"That's a happy thought," said Magus. "How do you survive with an outlook like that?"

"Vodka," responded Petrov.

"Anyway," said Magus, "I have a way out. Watch."

With far more drama then was required for the occasion, Magus reached into both his pockets and drew out his sword and staff.

"I'd like to make some kind of a joke about this," said Abda, "but I'm a bit stumped."

"Watch closely," responded Magus. "You might learn something." Then, Magus swept his sword, and with a whoosh of power, it cut through the bars twice, leaving a huge gap through which they could walk.

"Very impressive," said Kozhi as he walked into the cell block. "Willing to tell me how you managed to sneak those in?"

"What do you mean?" said Magus as he hid the sword and staff behind his back while acting as if there was no gaping hole in the bars.

"You know full well what I mean," responded the commander. "Now then, I have... a mutual friend to introduce you to. Shall you come, or do I need to use force?"

"No," said Magus, dropping his weapons.

"Very well," said the commander. "Follow me."

****

Magus and his allies were led through many twisting hallways, throughout which there were hallways leading off at random intervals. Eventually, they came to a room with a U-shaped dais. Figures cloaked in shadow stood at the top curve of the U, their eyes shining out like spotlights in the darkness. In front of them, directly between the two prongs of the U, was the G-Dwarf from before, looking impatient and checking his watch.

"*You!*" exclaimed Magus. "What are you doing here?"

"I have come to introduce you to my... associates," responded the G-Dwarf. "We have entered... a mutually beneficial agreement. I will forewarn you that any undue behavior shall not be accepted. We need... a figurehead. But remember, Mr. Breeman: figureheads can be replaced. Will you join us?"

"Perhaps," said Magus as he walked back to the center. "I don't trust you, but for that reason, it is obvious there is no other choice. We shall join you."

"A good choice," said the G-Dwarf. "The only one."

Then, one of the shadows leaned over and said "The Tzar has come to Smertnyhdrozhat' for the winter as is twadition. We need you to stwike so that we can seize contwol. Thewe are few guards, as most dwarves of dwaftable age are alweady on the fwont lines of the war. The Tzar's wooms are in the adamantine vein, and we need you to go there. The guards will change at twelve of the clock, and then he shall be alone. Find him, but wemember: we want him alive. No disintegwations."

"Allright," said Magus. "How much am I being paid for this?"

****

Magus grinned. Breaking into the winter palace was far easier than was expected. All he had to do was wave his sword in the general direction of a wall and it would fall to pieces. There were only three guards, but they probably wouldn't be interrupting anytime soon, being far too busy interrogating a bottle of absinthe. Now, having tunneled his way into the throne room, he was almost done with his ridiculous sidequest. The Tzar's throne room was gigantic but spartan, the only furnishings being a golden throne on which the Tzar sat. The Tzar himself was a rather skinny dwarf with purple plate mail, inscribed with gilt runes. Not the most intimidating of villains, but it could probably be worse.

"Who are you?" said the Tzar, his voice echoing throughout the gilded hall.

"Remember me?" asked Petrov, raising his axe.

"No," responded the Tzar. "Are you the new cook?"

"You don't remember what happened?" said Petrov. "You forgot about the *rytsar'* you exiled?"

"I exile all sorts of people these days," said the Tzar.

"The palace? During the Year of the Cave Swallow? On the fifth of May?"

"I exiled eight people that day."

"Eight!" exclaimed Magus. "Why would you do something like that?"

"Well someone spilled his soup on me, so I exiled him, his family, their families, his neighbors, the guy who delivers his newspapers, and a few bystanders who looked particularly shifty. What else do you expect me to do?"

"Forgive them?"

"Screw that!"

Magus simply stood and stared for a second. Before him was someone who on first glance would seem like a nice and kind man, yet would think nothing of ordering someone killed over the slightest infraction.

"Look," said Magus. "Will you get off your soapbox and stop telling people how I feel. I get it. The Tzar was bad. That still doesn't excuse the great purge, or any of the other things that came afterward. Besides, you haven't even had him kill anyone yet. All he's done is exile people."

Look, just kill him and we'll be done with it.

"Fine," said Magus, walking toward the Tzar and drawing his sword. Raising it over his head, Magus swung downward straight at the Tzar, hitting him in the head. The blade then bounced off.

"And they said the magic protections were a waste," stated the Tzar. "I'll have to have them executed. Now then: *Guards! Guards!*"

Magus felt a bead of sweat roll down his neck as the Tzar sat smirking. When the guards were roused from their drunken stupor he and his friends would be executed. There was no last minute plan, no hidden passage, and no *deus ex machina*. It was win or lose. Nothing more.

He paused for a moment, drawing in arcane strength before shouting, "Fascism capitalismus debilitata est!"

In one fell stroke, he cleaved the Tzar's head from his shoulders, slicing through not only flesh and bone, but the intricately carved armor and the throne behind it. As the guards rushed into the room an eternity too late, Magus picked up the Tzar's head and held it before him, shouting, "Your king is dead! The king is dead!"

Suddenly, everything stopped. Almost everything. Magus was still moving about normally, but everything else was still and grey.

"Mister Breeman," said the G-Dwarf. "You seem to have broken... Our agreement. You will have to be... punished. Really. You should have... foreseen... the consequences."

After that non sequitor, everything returned to normal. Now then, where were we?

Ah, yes.

"Your king is dead!" shouted Magus. "The Tzar has fallen!"

As the guards looked on Magus in shock and awe, one of them, evidently a brighter lad, simply looked at the head before saying, "*And?* That's why we have heirs."

"What do you mean?" said Magus. "I killed the king, now you have to surrender. That's how this kind of thing goes."

"If believing that makes you feel better, go ahead," responded the guard. "Now if you'll excuse us, we have to kill you now."

The guards rushed toward Magus, but they all stopped and fell to the ground, having been the target of a hex blasted across the room. As Magus walked past their contorted bodies, he heard a crash from a door behind the throne. As he rushed from the throne room and approached the adjoining balcony, he looked down and watched the dwarves in the square below erupting into turmoil between loyalists and revolutionaries.

Magus sighed. They had a lot of work to do.

Chapter 6
The Greater Purge

A lot of work had been done. So much, in fact, that it was amazing the party had managed to find time to sleep. It had been a harrowing year, and between counterrevolutionaries and outbreaks of famine, they hadn't expected to last the month. Despite that, there they stood: Petrov clad in a restored version of his older outfit, Ærin in ceremonial armor with runic sigils etched in gold, Abda wearing a suit he had acquired after pressing his talents into the field of espionage, and Magus wearing a blue woolen robe with naught but a few medals and a pair of gold lapels to betray its owner's status.

"Dammit!" swore Ærin as one of the decorative flanges on her scabbard hit her in the back of the leg for the umpteenth time. "I hate this armor. The gold decorations seem to have been alloyed with lead, the ornamental spikes make me look like a magnet dropped into a box of nails, and the gigantic pauldrons mean I can't get through a door without turning sideways! This entire ensemble is nothing but a waste of resources."

"Yes," said Petrov, "But you've got to admit it looks impressive. Besides, the waste isn't our fault. The propagandists insisted."

"We still share some of the responsibility," said Ærin. "It's gilt by association."

"Come on," said Petrov as they entered the council chamber and took their seats. Said seats were four smallish ones on the outer edge of the horseshoe shaped table. Ioseb—a large dwarf with a military coat and a luxurious beard who had been the General Secretary ever since the previous incumbent, Vladimir, had passed away the year before—was sitting at the head of the table, obviously waiting for something as the other members filed in.

"Hello," said Ioseb, standing up after everyone had entered. "This is the part where I kill you."

There were a few moments of stunned silence, and everyone stared at Ioseb in shock until one man burst into laughter. It started out a bit nervous, but it became more natural, and soon others joined in as well.

"I am not joking," said Ioseb. "You all are going to die."

The laughter was slightly more worried this time.

"I shall not speak thrice," stated Ioseb. "Guards, open fire."

Suddenly, Ioseb flickered and disappeared, revealed to be nothing more than an illusion. At the same time, holes were quickly opened in the steel walls, and nozzles of dark grey gunmetal were pushed through. They began to bark flame, spitting forth streams of lead into the room. Almost all of the council members were cut down in the first five seconds, but Magus managed to take cover behind the dais until the shooting was over.

Once the noise had stopped, Magus opened his eyes and saw the guards filing in, followed by the G-Dwarf. *Probably best to play dead,* he thought.

The G-Dwarf looked around at the bodies, and simply stated, "No one can know... Throw them into the atom smasher, and inform *Pravda* that most of the Soviet members were killed in an attack by the *bourgeoisie* scum. Ioseb will be pleased."

As Magus watched, the guards picked him up along with all the corpses and began to drag them away. He would have seen more, all of which would have cleared up several mysteries, but the guards dragged him by the legs, and the first time his head hit the stone floor, he decided to take a nice nap.

****

Magus woke up a few minutes later. This has no relevance at all to the story, as he forgot everything that happened for the next few minutes due to concussion-flavored amnesia. Head wounds are not to be taken lightly.

81

****

After a few more disruptions, Magus eventually came too for good. This was fortunate because at this point the guards were throwing him down a long, dark, chute. He landed rather roughly, but the pile of dead bodies cushioned his fall. Sitting up, he took stock, finding himself in desperate straits.

"I'll say," said Magus. "I can't believe how badly researched this book is!"

What?

"Assuming that Ioseb is intended to be an allegorical version of Stalin, (a fairly reasonable assumption given that Stalin was actually named Ioseb, with Joseph being the closest English approximation for Iosef, which was in turn the closest Russian approximation for Ioseb) then from his attempts to kill us it can be inferred that we are allegorical versions of Trotsky."

Did you just speak parentheses? How does that even work?

"However, there are several noticeable deviations from the historical record. While our killing of the Tzar while he was still in power instead of setting him on fire after he had already been dethroned can be written up to dramatic license, there's still a large number of inconsistencies. For starters, we have the fact that the Red Army consisted of just us, and you completely forgot about the White and Green armies. Furthermore, Trotsky was NOT assassinated while in the Soviet Union, nor was it blamed on foreign capitalists. Instead-"

Hey, look! A distraction!

At that point there was a great banging and cursing, which grew louder and louder until eventually Ærin fell out of the bottom of the shaft. She still had her armor on, and fortunately the guards forgot to remove Kettlingr.

"At last!" shouted Ærin in joy as she got up and removed her pauldrons, which fell to the ground, squashing a few rats. "Freedom!"

"Wait," said Magus. "Did she even get Kettlingr back to begin with? I don't remember seeing it after the start of chapter four."

She got it back off-screen, okay! A wizard did it.

"What, do you lunatics think wizards just go around, changing the fabric of reality for no reason?"

Yes.

"Why?"

Because that's what wizards do.

"Look!" shouted Petrov as he crawled out of the pile of corpses and pointed to the wall. "Stop bickering. We have bigger problems."

Magus's gaze inevitably followed Petrov's finger across the floor— covered in grimy water that looked as if it could contain a tentacle demon or two despite the fact that it was only an inch deep—up the rusted, groaning, wall slowly sliding outwards, and over to the—

"Wait a minute," said Magus "The moving wall?"

Oh, yeah, I forgot to mention that earlier. Yeah, the walls are moving in.

"By Hecate's tits!" shouted Magus. "Were you trying to get us killed?"

Maybe...

"Dear Jupiter, how are we supposed to get out of this?"

"Well," responded Ærin, "we could try that door over there."

"Don't be an idiot," said Magus. "What kind of moron puts a door in a trash compactor?"

"The kind of moron that's OSHA compliant?" responded Ærin.

****

"All right," said Ærin, "I remember this level from that time we went on a propaganda march. Had to shake a bunch of people's hands and stuff. I think the exits should be right about... here."

Magus looked around at the square room Ærin had found. There were no doors other than the one they had entered in by, and no features other than the six statues in the center made of an eldritch black metal. All gleamed and were free of rust, and each depicted a humanoid figure in spiked armor wielding a sword engraved with intricate runes.

As Magus's gaze passed over the one in the center, the door slammed closed and the statues jumped to life, raising their weapons and rushing at the party.

"It's a trap!" shouted Magus.

"Well that's obvious," responded Abda. "You didn't need to shout."

"Yes I did," responded Magus. "It was to add dramatic tension."

"Look," said Petrov as his axe lashed out, clattering off one statue's armor. "Can we focus on the matter at hand?"

"Why?" responded Magus. "They're solid chunks of metal. There's nothing we can do to them. They have no vital organs to stab, no arteries to puncture, no groins to kick! It's hopeless."

"Dammit, Magus!" shouted Petrov as he ducked a mighty blow. "I've been adventuring for nigh on a hundred years, and I know my clichés. You just found that sword a little while ago, and that means it'll be the only weakness these dungeon's monsters have. Get over here!"

"I can't go into melee!" responded Magus. "I'm a mage! I might as well just slit my throat! At least it'll be painless that way."

"Yes, you're a mage," said the sword, "but I'm a magic sword!"

"First," said Magus, "you're a sword, and swords can't talk. Second, I don't know the first thing about fighting!"

"I propose to teach you," responded the sword.

"Look," said Magus, "isn't there some other way we can do this?"

"How about this?" said the sword. Magus's arm rose, bringing the sword to his own neck. "You do what I say, and I don't cut your head off."

"Well, when you put it like that," responded Magus, "is there any chance of you doing the fighting for me?"

"All you need to do is relax," said the sword. "Just relax, and let your instincts... take... control."

****

"That was the most impressive slaughter I have ever seen," said Petrov, "and the amazing bit is that we were on the winning side!"

"It slices, it dices!" said the sword. "Call now and you get an extra twelve gallon barrel of kickass absolutely free!"

"Quiet," said Magus. "I really hate having to reuse lines."

"Then stop reusing them!" said the sword. "Just accept that I can talk and be done with it."

"Why would I need to accept that you can talk?" said Magus. "You're a sword, so you can't."

"You've seen me talk!" shouted the sword. "How can you continue to deny it?"

"Because," said Magus, "I have faith that you can't, and so you can't."

"*Helloooo?*" responded the sword. "Elder Earth to Magus? Reality doesn't work like that!"

"Est nunc verum," said Magus, waving a hand, which burst into purple flame that engulfed the sword and silenced its cries.

"Now then," said Magus, turning to face his friends, "where were we?"

"We were at the bit where you just *silenced the one thing that was giving us useful advice!*" shouted Ærin.

"What advice?" said Magus. "It was my idea to jump into the melee."

"No," said Ærin. "It was Petrov's idea for you to use the sword, and it was the sword that convinced you to fight."

"That's stupid," said Magus. "Swords can't talk. Where did you get that idea?"

"From the fact that it talks," said Ærin.

"That doesn't prove a thing," Said Magus. Suddenly, as if reality itself was tired of the characters' inane bickering, a crashing noise came from the middle distance as one of the walls burst in and began to hemorrhage dwarves.

"See!" shouted the sword. "I told you to listen to my advice!"

"Hey!" shouted Magus. "I thought I had silenced you! That spell should have lasted for a year and a day!"

"It's still working," said the sword. "Think about what it does."

"It silences an enemy without killing them by immobilizing their... vocal cords..." responded Magus.

"Look!" shouted Petrov, as he dodged an axe swing. "Could you help a little here?"

"Fine," said Magus. "IMMOBILES!"

As he shouted out his words, a purple glow appeared around his hands and lashed out at the dwarves, stiffening their joints and freezing their muscles. Suddenly, as soon as it appeared, the spell burst and the dwarves rushed back into action.

"Dammit!" shouted Magus. "Spell resistance! It's almost as if the universe is trying to create some kind of balance between those who can shape the fabric of reality with their mind and those who can't."

Magus sighed and then jumped into the fray, slashing his sword straight through one of the dwarves' steel shields. Then, as abruptly as it had begun, the onrush of dwarves stopped. The remaining solders retreated from the room.

"Come on," said Magus. "Let's follow them. With luck, we'll make it back to civilization."

"Why?" said Ærin. "Everyone will be on the lookout for us back there!"

"Because," responded Magus, "we're regarded as heroes there. Didn't you hear what Ioseb told the guards to say to the media? All we have to do is say it was cover for a secret mission. Besides, if I'm right, we ought to be near *Obshchiĭport*."

"You mean-" said Ærin.

"Shush," said Magus. "We don't want to spoil it for the readers."

****

"Are you sure this is a good idea?" said Ærin.

"Yes," responded Magus. "Also, thank you for changing your section-starting statement of doubt."

"Variety is the spice of life."

"Curry powder is the spice of rice," interjected Petrov.

"That was a horrible joke," responded Magus. "Never say that again."

"Sorry," apologized Petrov, "but we were running low on our inane bickering quota."

"Look," said Abda. "Can we just establish the scene and move on!"

Fine. Magus looked around the bay that gave *Obshchiĭport* its name, seeing several ironclad warships being assembled by an ancient technique, of which no man has ever heard. Or woman. Up till now, at any rate. Magus saw that one of them—the largest—was not only finished, but soon to leave drydock. It was called the *Sevastopol*.

"That one," he said. "That one's mine."

"*Ours,*" said the rest of the team simultaneously.

****

"All right," said Magus, climbing onto the ship. "We're commandeering this vessel."

"*Innnnntttttttrrrrrruuuuuddeeeer!*" shouted the guard Magus had spoken to. If it weren't for a quick bit of spell work, Magus's guts would have been spilled all over the deck.

"All right," said Magus, "let's try that again."

****

"I am Magus the Blue," exclaimed Magus, stepping atop the conning tower. "I am the hero of the dwarves. I have come to take command of this ship."

"Wait," said the captain. "*Pravda* said you were dead!"

"That's just cover for my secret mission," responded Magus. "And for it I need this ship. We shall launch immediately, but first take down the radio antenna in case of an attack by capitalist antenna rats. If it calls us traitors before you take it down, ignore it lest we fall into the antenna rats' evil plan."

"Very well," responded the captain. "Crew, prepare the ship, and take down that antenna!"

As the crew ran about doing various things, Magus pulled a tricorn hat out of his pointy hat, put his pointy hat inside the tricorn hat before putting it on his head.

"All right," said Magus. "It's time to set sail."

****

"Miiiissssttteeeerrrr Bbbbbbrrrrrreeeeeemmmmmaaaaannnn," said the G-Dwarf, walking up behind Magus as he searched through a chest in a rather small, sealed room in the belly of the ship.

Magus turned to the G-Dwarf, completely unsurprised by his entrance into the locked room.

"I realize this may not be the most convenient moment for a heart to heart," the G-Dwarf continued, "but I had to ask... Did you really think you could escape us?"

"Yes," responded Magus, pulling something out of the chest. "Look around you."

"Wait!" shouted out the G-Dwarf as he noticed the rearranged floor panels and the detonator in Magus's hand. "Y-you can't do this! There are rules!"

"And?" asked Magus. "We're breaking them."

"You need me! If I'm dead, you'll die too!"

"Perhaps," responded Magus as he pushed the button. "But whether we live or die, it shall be by our own hands."

****

As the dust from the explosion settled, a charred piece of paper wafted down, probably protected from the explosion by the G-Dwarf's metallic briefcase. It was an identification card listing who the dwarf was and who he worked for. The picture alone was probably worth millions.

Magus snapped his fingers, which sparked with a violet glow. As the paper began to kindle, he knew there was one thing that had to be said.

"Goodbye. I don't think we'll be seeing each other again."

****

Subject: Magus Breeman
Status: Rogue
Addendum: Subject is highly intelligent and resourceful.
Avoid at all costs.

****

Chapter 7
Odin for the Æsir, And Pain for the Elves.

"Land ho!" shouted Magus, with far more enthusiasm than any sane being should have.

"Look," said Petrov, watching the coastline to the starboard side "I know it's been boring here for the past few days, but there's nothing else we can do. If we circle north around the continent we risk running into the Maelstrom, so instead we have to circle south around Elminghiem and Artoria in order to get to the nearest friendlies."

"Yes," said Magus, "but—"

Suddenly, almost out of the blue, there was the shrieking sound of tearing metal coming from the port side of the ship. It continued for a long, drawn out second, and then ceased as quickly as it had begun. Magus rushed over to the side the sound had come from, but there was nothing there but a gaping hole sliced into the hull, and an empty patrol boat bobbing along nearby.

"Dammit!" shouted Magus. "Whoever it was, he's already inside."

"Don't worry sir," responded the captain. "We'll catch him."

****

Obshchiĭ K. Rubashke, private first class, was worried. He had joined the military out of loyalty to his country, but now he was on a ship out in the middle of the ocean, far away from the battlefront. Worse yet, he had heard that there was actually a chance their mission was not sanctioned by their glorious leader, and that Magus, the hero of the rebellion, might actually be a traitor. Despite the size of the introduction he has been given, none of this will matter in three minutes and forty seconds.

Step, step, step.

Three minutes now.

Step, step, step.

Three minutes, fifty nine—

...

Are you sure I've done this before?

...

Oh, all right. I'll skip to the good bit then.

****

As Magus paced along the deck, waiting for the underlings to go and do all of the work for him, merely a few feet below him, danger lurked. Well, not lurked. Idled maybe. Loitered. One dwarf. And another. They shall differentiate in the following ways: One shall talk like Rambo, and the other shall not, one shall be tied up, and the other shall not, and one shall be awesome, and the other shall not.

"Well?" said the one. "Are you ready to tell me where they are?"

"Never!" shouted the other. "When my comrades catch you, they'll feed you to the dogs."

"No," responded the one. "You abandoned your countrymen the instant you left port."

"Nonsense," said the other, struggling against his bonds. "I am as loyal to comrade Ioseb as any other man."

"Really?" queried the first as he raised his gleaming blade. "As loyal as any man perhaps, but what about any *dwarf?*"

****

"What's taking them so long?" exclaimed Magus. "That was a small boat, so odds are there's only one man!"

"Yes," said Petrov, "But I'm pretty sure the Tzar said the same thing about you."

"Yes," responded Magus, "But that's different. I'm the main character. I get to do that kind of thing."

"How do you know that?" responded Ærin. "For all you know, this is some kind of overly drawn out prologue to introduce the main character."

"Yes," said Magus. "But how would we identify him? Look at what happened to that girl back on page two! The replacement could come from anywhere!"

"True," interjected Abda, "but if I had to make a guess, I would say that the replacement would be—"

Suddenly, as if reality itself was conspiring to end the conversation before the meta-gaming could spread, a dwarf fully armored in adamantine plate ripped up through the deck, eviscerating a crewman who was unfortunate enough to be walking nearby. As the nearby marines opened fire, the menacing figure simply laughed as the bullets flattened themselves and ricocheted off his blue metal armor. There was not a single point for anything to get in, as even the dwarf's face was protected by an angry, scowling mask.

Magus jumped backwards in shock, realizing that there was soon to be an opening for main character, and that—

"I CAST FIREBALL!"

What? You can't do that! That's cheating!

"Why? It's a perfectly valid spell."

Yes, but this is supposed to be a climatic occasion!

"It was. It just was a quick one."

Fine. The fireball lanced out, and the dwarf blocked it with the shield he had all along that I didn't make up on the spot and just happened to not mention until now.

"I hate you."

Glad to hear it. Anyway, as the armor-clad dwarf rushed forward, Magus drew his sword, knowing that he would only have one chance to survive. As soon as the dwarf reached him, Magus used his sword with one hand to shove-parry the axe, while he used his staff in the other to ram a thaumic charge through the mask's eyehole.

"There," said Magus. "Done with the boss fight. Can we get on with the inane bickering now?"

"Not yet," said the captain. "Bad news. The Eternity Engine was damaged when he hacked in, and we don't have the ability to repair it. We've still got the diesel backups, but we'll be lucky if those get us to shore."

"Let me guess," responded Magus. "The nearest land is hostile and we're going to have to beach the ship and fight our way through several miles worth of bad guys before we get to escape."

"Not really," responded the captain. "I figured we could sit around and die of starvation, but your idea sounds better."

"Looks like the decision's been made for us," said Ærin. "Look: Boats."

"Boats!" shouted Petrov. "But that means—"

"Elves," interjected the captain. "Fire off the starboard bow!"

At the captain's command, the cannons began to blaze, but as the missiles arced toward their target, a greenish, tangible light began to rise

95

from the water, forming a protective dome around the enemy and shielding them from harm. Not even the sails had been damaged.

"Brace yourselves!" shouted Magus. "They're going to ram us!"

As the elvish ships drew closer, Magus got a good long look at the odd, organic hull and the seamless, polished deck before the hulls smacked together with the groan of bending steel.

As polished steel ground against magically hardened wood, a number of prick-eared boarders jumped over onto the dwarvish ship with alien grace, brandishing otherworldly crystalline blades, glowing with a vile green light. The defenders fought well, but in the end, there was only one way it could go.

****

"Now what?"

"Look!" shouted Magus. "Will you stop saying that? You repeat the same thing every time we cut to a new scene!"

"And?" said Ærin. "I'll stop complaining about your leadership when you lead us to somewhere we can't complain about."

She gestured with her left hand, rattling their chains as she pointed to their once-more dismal surroundings.

As a departure from the standard cell, everything, including the chains, was made out of magically hardened wood, but other than that it was standard to all the other cells throughout this book, presumably having been stamped out somewhere in China.

"Must we continue with this charade?" said Magus with a sigh. "I'm just going to reach into my pocket, pull out my sword, and slice through the bars."

Try it.

After the narrator's encouragement, Magus reached into his pocket for his sword, and it only took him two tries to realize it was gone. He sighed and sat down, resigned to the railroading.

****

As the prisoners were being led off into the distance, Magus looked out on the sea of tree huts, each individually carved from the living wood, and he saw why the elves had managed to spare so many swordsmages for capturing just one ship. They were everywhere. The boarding party was not some kind of elite task force, but simply an average group of raiders.

As Magus gaped in awe, a dark shape descended from the sky, scattering mages and slaves alike. As a smaller, more pedestrian shadow got off of the first shadow's back; Magus shuddered, as he began to feel a presence he had only fought once before.

"Hello," said Aragon. "I've been waiting to see you."

****

Nine lights, rushing through the darkness. One light falls into shadow. Now there are naught but eight.

****

A bright light shined in Magus's eyes, created by an eldritch flame that did little to illuminate the room and just barely allowed Magus to see the chair he was strapped to. As he struggled and squirmed, Aragon paced back and forth in front of him, spitting questions and then ignoring the answers he got.

"Why are you here?" he snapped.

"I told you!" said Magus desperately. "We were betrayed by Ioseb and our ship was raided while we were passing the Cape of No Hope!"

97

"You're lying!" screamed Aragon. "There's no way you could have gotten so far inside the defense net without protection. Who was helping you?"

"I told you," shouted Magus. "No-one!"

"*Silence!*" screeched Aragon.

Magus sighed as he wondered why all of the villains were about as eloquent as a budgerigar with Tourette's.

"I heard that!" snapped Aragon. "I don't know how you managed to hide the knowledge of your employer from me, but I can still read your surface thoughts."

"I'm able to do it because I wasn't hired by anyone!" shouted Magus.

"Lies," hissed Aragon. "I saw what the G-Dwarf could do. There's no way you would have been able to destroy him."

"But I did!" protested Magus. However, even as he said the words, something rang false about them. Why would a being powerful enough to halt time allow itself to be killed? For that matter, how would you even go about killing one?

"Hrm," said Aragon. "So perhaps you tried to kill him after all. No matter. Your fate shall be the same either way. Guards! Take him to Cyanesque!"

Almost immediately after Aragon shouted, two guards in scale mail and white surcoats marched in, grabbed Magus, and then marched out.

****

Eight lights, walking through the shadows. One falters, straying from the others as it turns to black. Now there are naught but seven.

****

"Hey!" shouted Magus as the guard shoved him along the wooden corridor. "Would you mind being a bit gentler? You almost bruised me there."

"Hrmmm…" pondered the guard as he punched Magus in the chest. "Yes, I would mind. Sorry if that bothers you."

As Magus wheezed and fell over, he saw out of the corner of his eye a few prisoners following an odd looking guard. Among other things, his beard stretched down to his knees, although that wasn't saying much given that he was only four feet tall. The bearded guard raised a finger to his lips, warning Magus to keep quiet, before imbedding a battleaxe in Magus's guard's back.

"Hello," said Petrov. "Need some help?"

****

"But how did you guys get out?" asked Magus.

"We waited until the guard was asleep," said Petrov, "and then we slit his throat and took his ears."

"You cut off his ears?" said Magus. "That's sick!"

"And?" responded Petrov. "How else do you expect me to masquerade as an elf?"

"Just put a helmet on!" said Magus. "No one would be able to see your ears!"

"You can't!" said Petrov. "They'll know! The ears have lumps of Aether in them! They're what makes an elf an elf! Without them, they lose their psychic powers. You put them on and they'll assume that you're one of them!"

"Do you have any proof?" asked Magus.

99

"That guard didn't notice me, did he?"

****

"Rejoice!" proclaimed Magus as he swung open the door to the prison cell. "You are free!"

Magus's entrance would have probably been impressive, if anyone there could see it. Regrettably, the only person in the cell was a blind, elderly man. He was gaunt, but his baggy clothes stated he had once been rather portly. His face was a mass of wrinkles, and his eyes were gone, replaced with festering, blackened pits.

"Freedom?" he said. "There is no freedom. I shall never be at peace."

"What do you mean?" asked Magus. "There is always hope. They can take your sight, but they can't touch your mind."

"But they can," responded the man. "They laid a geas on me many years ago."

"Wait," said Magus. "What do birds have to do with this?"

"It's G-E-A-S, not G-E-E-S-E," snapped the old man. "Thanks to their magic, I have been bound as surely as if I had been tied down with chains. I can no longer even think of leaving the grove without undergoing terrible pain."

"Why are you here?" asked Magus.

"I..," said the old man, apparently caught in the past. "I did what I had to do. They were going to kill my daughter. They had no intention to do so, but she would have died just the same. I was forced to kill a man in order to save her, and when his comrades caught up with us, I was blinded and sent here. I sat around for what felt like years, until one day, they wove a spell to return my vision for a few days. I saw her then. Beautiful. I cried at the sight, for the spells stopped her from noticing me, and I knew that I would never be able to see her again. Years passed. Empires fell.

Monuments crumbled. Secrets were lost. Once, there were many trapped in here. Now, there is just me. Me and the darkness."

"Is there anything we can do for you?" asked Magus.

"Kill me," said the man.

Magus reached into his pocket, discovering that whatever magic kept his sword from returning to his person had vanished. Pulling out the sword, he looked at it, looked at the prisoner, and then lowered his blade.

"I'm sorry," he said. "I can't bring myself to do it. I can't kill an unarmed man."

"All right," said Petrov as he cut the old man's head off. "More kills for me."

****

"Now what?" said Ærin.

"What do you mean 'now what?'" shouted Magus. "We're out of the village, isn't that enough?"

"No," said Ærin. "It's not enough. "We're hopelessly lost, and we don't even know which way is north!"

"Actually," said Petrov, "we do know where we are. North by 34, West by 37."

"How do you know?" asked Abda.

"GPS," responded Petrov as he spit out a bit of dirt. "Geological Piquancy Sampling."

****

"Look," said Ærin after another segue. "It's not where we are that I'm worried about, it's where we're going. The nearest friendly country is Psudor, and they're seven leagues away."

"Don't worry," said Magus. "We'll head to Artoria. There are some bad stories about the place, but odds are they're empire propaganda."

Chapter 8
And Yet It Moves

"'Empire propaganda,' you said. 'Probably nice people,' you said."

"Look," responded Magus. "It was this or go through the empire itself, and we're wanted men over there."

"*And?*" responded Ærin. "We're wanted over here, too! Out of all the countries to hide in, you had to choose the one that worships elves. I was almost burned at the stake. Burned. At. The. God. Damn. *Stake.*"

They had arrived at a small village two days ago, and although the people were poor, one of them was glad to share a room in his hut. Things had gone well until Magus had said that he was a mage, and everyone in the room went quiet. When prompted, Magus proved it by pulling a Ping-Pong ball out of the host's ear. The man had recoiled in shock, and soon the townspeople were taking out the kindling. It went downhill from there.

From what they heard during the speeches before their execution, all magic was banned in the country, except for that which came from the elves, and as usual, the penalty for breaking such rules was death.

It was close. If Magus hadn't pulled out some quick spell work at the last minute, they would have been adventurer flambé. Now they were wandering the wilderness, vaguely hoping the enemy would forget they were there.

"All right," said Ærin. "We get it. Stop it with the flashback, already."

"No," said Magus as the world went gray.

They were back in Nam again. He had only spent a few weeks there, but in that time he would find his core beliefs threatened. It all started when Charlie—

"You haven't even been to Vietnam!" shouted Ærin.

"I know that," said Magus. "But the scene needed some spiffing up."

Just then, almost if the gods themselves were attempting to force them to cease their inane bickering, several knights on horseback galloped over the nearby hill, surrounding the heroes with a wall of horseflesh.

Just as Magus had given himself up for lost, the circling stopped and one knight, wearing a bucket helm and a white surcoat emblazoned with a red sword dismounted, walked up to the party, and cleared his throat.

"Ahem," he coughed. "What is your name?"

Magus found his throat had locked up in fright, but he just barely managed to squeeze out "Magus Bree-" before the crusader waved his hand and cut Magus off.

There were a few moments of silence as the knight mused over what he had heard, but after several seconds he shook his head and asked, "What is your favorite colour?"

"Blue," Magus squeaked.

"All right," said the crusader. "This is the hard one: what is the occult name for the formula $\Gamma(z) = \int_0^\infty t^{z-1} e^{-t} dt = \frac{e^{-\gamma z}}{z} \prod_{k=1}^\infty \left(1 + \frac{z}{k}\right)^{-1} e^{z/k}$, $\gamma \approx 0.577216$?"

"Ooh!" exclaimed Magus. "I know this one! It's the gamma function!" Then, after looking around, he realized what he had said and shouted "No, wait—I didn't mean that!"

"Of course you didn't," said the Templar. "None of the mages we capture mean to say it. I'm rather sorry about this, but I'm afraid we're going to have to kill you."

"Please!" wailed Magus, dropping down to his knees as he abandoned all pretensions of dignity. "Don't burn me! I have so much left to live for!"

"What?" said the crusader, drawing back indignantly. "Burn you? What do you think we are, barbarians?"

Magus breathed a sigh of relief, but it was short-lived as the Templar continued.

"We're going to have you hung, drawn, and quartered," he said. "Much more civilized that way."

****

"Congratulations on your illustrious leadership," said Ærin. "Did you know this is the seventh time you've gotten us captured?"

"What else did you expect me to do?" asked Magus. "Look outside this iron cart. There's a whole army out there."

"Just kill them," suggested the sword. "There's only... sixty nine thousand, one hundred and thirty five of them. Piece of cake."

"Yes," said Magus, "but in this case the cake is made out of lead and arsenic."

"What about magic?" asked Abda. "Can't you could turn us invisible or something?"

"No," said Magus dejectedly. "I tried messing about with that kind of thing when I was a kid. Almost blinded myself. Not really worth the trouble."

"Can you brainwash one of the guards?" asked Ærin.

"Well," said Magus. "There is the thirteenth rune, but I don't want to use that."

"Why not?" asked Abda.

"Because," said Magus. "It's supposed to be used as a love spell and-"

"And *why* do you have that prepared?" interjected Ærin.

"No reason."

"Good."

****

Magus's head nodded as he bumped up and down in his new cell, an iron cubicle mounted on a cart, lit by only a flicker of light shining through the hole in the door.

"Congratulations on your amazing plan," said Abda from the next box over. "It'll be much easier to escape now that they shifted us to maximum security."

"What do you mean, *my* plan?" shouted Magus. "This was *Ærin's* idea!"

"*Hey!*" interjected Ærin. "Leave me out of this! You're the one who screwed up the spell! Besides, Abda was the one who brought up magic in the first place!"

"*And?*" shouted Abda. "*You* were the one who bumped into Magus during the casting. Why are you blaming me?"

As the bickering continued, Magus sighed and leaned against the wall, wondering who decided to give cells too small to sit down in such low roofs. Judging by all the rattling the cart was doing, it was probably the same person who thought triangular was a good shape for a wheel.

****

Sitting in the darkness under a craggy rock were two of what appeared to be children, snuggled up in the same bedroll, presumably for warmth. As they slept, a creepy, ominous figure crept down from the outcrop above them, reaching for the neck of the smaller of the two. He probably would have succeeded had it not been for the fact that the sleepers were not asleep at all. As is, it got the thief a sword through the gut.

"Did you have to kill him?" said the skinnier of the two.

"Yes," said the shorter and fatter one. "He was going to kill us!"

"I know that," responded Tall, "But couldn't you have knocked him out, or something?"

"Yes," said Fat, "But that would have taken too long. Tell me though, would a bit of buggery cheer you up?"

"Would it ever!" exclaimed Tall.

****

The iron cart slid into a walled city of stone and wood, its three-sided wheels clanking as the horses dragged it across the cobblestones under the shadow of the towering, gothic keep. Regrettably, all of this was lost on Magus because the window into his cell was one inch wide.

****

"All right," said the sword as it returned to its accustomed place in Magus's pocket. "That's enough. We're breaking out."

"You again?" responded Magus. "I thought the author had forgotten you existed."

"Whatever gave you that idea?" asked the sword. "Anyway, we're leaving. Pull me out so I can cut through the bars."

"Sorry," said Magus. "My hands are tied. There's an anti-magic field on this cell, and I can't get to my staff to break through it."

"And?" said the sword. "My sharpness isn't magic, and my sentience is powerful enough to avoid being dispelled. Just pull me out and cut your way through."

"I'll try," said Magus as he shuffled around in his bonds. "I'm sorry," he said after a moment of effort, "but they're tied behind my back, so there isn't much I can do."

"What do you mean 'they're'?" asked the sword. "There's no one in here but us."

"My *hands,*" said Magus. "They're tied."

There was a moment of silence.

"If I had limbs," said the sword, "I would strangle you."

"If I wasn't tied up right now, I would too," responded Magus.

The sword stared at Magus for a bit, which was a very impressive feat given that it lacked eyes.

"You're going to pay for this," said the sword.

"I'm sorry," said Magus, "but I'm running out of things to do. Would you mind throwing me a rope?"

"You and I both know that Hell exists," responded the sword, "and for those jokes, you are going there."

"Can't do that," said Magus. "This yarn's dragging on enough without adding backtracking to the mix."

"If we get out of here," said the sword, "I will kill you, find a cleric to resurrect you, and then kill you again, just to make you pay for all the puns."

"Why?" asked Magus. "Don't you find my jokes punny?"

"Does the fact that I'm trying to fall over and slit your throat give you a clue?" responded the sword.

"I know the jokes are annoying," said Magus, "But I need something to fill time until the guards throw us in the pungeon."

"There shall be a reckoning," said the sword. "You can count on that."

"I usually count on my fingers," said Magus, "but if they drag me by the cuffs I'm afraid such things shall be a bit above my head."

"Oh dear Narrator," said the sword, futilely attempting to kneel, "Our father who art in heaven, please deliver me from this idiot and his mind numbing jests."

Sorry, but I'm paid by the word. Magus, wool you keep it up for a bit? I don't want publishers to think I've been flax.

"Actually," said Magus, "I'm almost at the end of my rope—*argh!*"

"I warned him," said the sword. "He really should have listened."

****

As the two nameless and faceless guards unloaded the iron cells from the cart, there was a clang inside the nearest as a bluemetal sword pierced straight through the wall of the cell, decapitating one of the guards and hiding its metallic sheen under a layer of gore.

"Thanks for the promotion," said the remaining guard.

"Don't mention it," muttered the sword.

****

"You really ought to be more careful," said Magus to the sword, now carried on the back of the newly solitary guard. "You almost killed me there!"

"Believe me," said the sword, its voice dripping with sarcasm.[4] "That was unintentional."

"Now wha—"

"Look," said Magus, rudely interrupting Ærin in the middle of her catchphrase, "I know that your catchphrase has become the narrator's standard way to lead into a description of the new location, but it's ceased being annoying and become an excuse for homicide."

"Will you be quiet?" shouted the nameless redshirt. "I'm trying to look intimidating here!"

"*And?*" said Magus. "Look around you. We're the only ones here."

"*And?*" said the guard. "This may look like an empty corridor, but there might be someone invisible in here, and if so I want to look my best."

"That," replied Magus, "Is the most idiotic thing I've ever heard."

"Shut up," responded the guard. "Prisoners aren't allowed to speak."

"And?" responded Magus. "What will you do if I don't? Chop my head off? Oh, wait, you're already going to do that."

"Wellllll..." said the guard reluctantly, "I've got a bit of a busy schedule today, but I think I could manage to book us some time in the torture chambers."

"Shutting up," said Magus.

****

---

[4] And blood. Don't forget the blood.

"Wow," said Magus as the party was lead into the torture chamber. "That's a huge rack."

"I know," responded the guard. "It used to be smaller, but I paid to have it enlarged. We've got a special furnace too, so our implements are always hot and—"

Regrettably, the guard's tirade of innuendoes was halted as Petrov burst out into laughter, earning him a speech and a stern look.

"Oh, think I'm funny, do you?" said the guard. "How about we take you over to room 101 and see if you're still laughing afterward."

"What's in there?" queried Petrov. "A huge rooster? Perhaps someone named Richard?"

"You know what's in room 101," responded the guard. "*Everyone* knows what's in room 101. Room 101 contains the worst thing in the world."

"More innuendos, then?" said Petrov sarcastically.

"That's it," said the guard, grabbing Petrov's chains and dragging him over to a door in the nearby wall. "You're going in."

"Ah, well," said Petrov. "Can't be as bad as your breath."

"Really?" asked the guard. "I wouldn't be so sure about that."

As the guard dragged the dwarf over to the door, Magus's eyes were inexorably drawn to that dread portal. As it opened, he looked into the darkness beyond, wondering what it was that Petrov could see. As he watched in horror, Petrov's skin turned deathly pale. As the poor fool fainted, Magus gasped in shock, wondering what could scare one such as him. When the dwarf was finally dragged back, his face contorted into silent screams of pain. As his spasms ceased, he began to wheeze as if he was attempting to articulate something but could not find the breath.

"What was it?" said Magus, bending down in order to hear. "What do they have in there?"

Petrov moaned before looking at Magus and saying naught but one word.

"Cats."

****

"*Cats!*" shouted Magus as they were dragged off to the audience chamber. "You told them everything in order to escape a room full of *cats?* What the hell is wrong with you?"

"I have every right to fear them," responded Petrov. "Those beasts have destroyed many a mine and slain many a foe."

"No," responded Magus, "they haven't."

"*You're like a bunch of children!*" shouted the guard, annoyed that the session in the torture chambers had not intimidated the party. "Will you please just shut up?"

"I don't wanna," said Magus.

"This is for your own good," said the guard. "You are soon to be in the audience of Fredrick the Third, Lord of Artoria and King of the Nine Realms. He is a Cleric of the Twentieth level, and could snuff out your petty lives in an instant if so he wished."

"If he's as competent as the torturers," said Magus, "I doubt he has enough magic to boil a pot of water. Guy's probably lucky if he can snuff out the life of a mayfly."

"*Silence!*" screeched the guard.

"How very eloquent of you," responded Magus. "Perhaps you could try saying something else. The readers are starting to lose interest."

"*Silence!*"

"No."

****

As the guard shoved Magus into the throne room, a booming voice from the muscular man on the throne in the center of the dais at the back of the room shouted, "Who dares disturb Fredrick, The Great and Powerful?"

"I dare," responded Magus. "You may have an army of bullyboys, but as far as supernatural ability goes, you've got the firepower of a drunken hamster."

"You shall fear me," responded the voice, "Because I am Fredrick, The Great and Powerful."

"Broken record much?" responded Magus. "Show us where the curtain you're hiding behind is, and I'll let you live."

"There is no curtain," said the man on the dais. "This is me!"

"Oh," said Magus, disappointedly. "Are you sure?"

"*Yes!*" shouted the man on the dais, apparently annoyed at the idiocy of the story's characters.

Getting up from his throne, he walked down the length of the room toward them. "You. Are. Going. To. Die. Please do take this seriously."

"Why?" asked Magus as he pulled out his sword. "Tell me, has anyone ever seen past the illusion you put up?"

"What illusion?" said the man.

"This one," responded Magus, throwing his sword vaguely sideward. Despite all logic that things should happen otherwise, the sword stopped in midair and stuck. As the party watched, a patch of red spread from it, and as it began to grow, it left behind patches of color in the shape of an elderly man who had fallen prone. Meanwhile, the man standing before them flickered and disappeared as if he had never been.

"See?" said Magus. "Simple problem, simple solution."

"Yes," said Ærin, "but..."

"What?" said Magus; despite the fact that he was sure he knew what she was going to say.

"What now?" said Ærin.

Close enough.

"Do you think this is over?" asked a voice that seemed to come from everywhere at once. "Do you really think the chapter's going to end?"

"No," said Magus, "but I rather wish it was."

"Don't worry," said the voice. "It will be soon. OPHANIM, HEAR MY CALL!"

As the voice spoke, an eldritch glow filled the room, and faint ethereal voices began to speak, whispering praise in a language that was old when the stars were new. As the susurrus grew louder, the building began to shake, as if the world itself was moving at the speaker's whim. With the whisperings growing louder every second, the air itself began to writhe and boil, as if seen through a warped glass, and the entire room began to glow with a blinding white light.

As the miniature sun in the epicenter of the effects began to brighten, Magus had to look away, shielding his eyes from the blinding glare. Then, as suddenly as they began, the voices stopped. When Magus looked up, he

113

saw that the sun had vanished, replaced by multicolored wheels with eyes looping around the rim, seemingly taken directly from a hippie's acid induced nightmare.

"Hullo," said one of the apparitions. "Tell me, are you Magus Breeman?"

"Y-yes..," said Magus hesitantly. "I am he. Why do you wish to know?"

"Various reasons," responded the ocular hula hoops. "Please excuse me, as I must confer with my fellows."

After a moment of silence in which the Ophanim remained stationary, they began to circle again. Blue lightning crackled between them, flashing from rim to rim.

"I'm sorry about this," said the one who appeared to be the spokesman of the group. "But I'm afraid we have to kill you."

"Why?" asked Magus, attempting to stall as he edged toward the door. "If you do kill me," he added, "I'll be sorry about it, too."

"I really wish it could be some other way," said the glowing wheel. "We've got orders from up top, and the last guy to ignore them ended up burning."

As the sparking between the Ophanim began to glow brighter and brighter, Magus sighed and began to hide his face behind his arm for the second time in so many pages. Then, suddenly, it stopped.

"What, again?" said Magus, clearly overwhelmed by the sheer epicness of the narration.

Magus stared blankly for a moment before saying, "I would appreciate if you would refrain from putting words in my mouth, as well as trying to give me emotions that are not my own."

No. Anyway, as Magus looked up from the spreading yellow stain in his robes—

"Keep that up and I'll kill you."

Have fun with that. Anyway, after looking up, Magus saw that the wheels had ceased their spinning, and were looking at him with inquisitive eyes.

"Sorry about that," said the one in the lead. "Transmission was garbled. Apparently there was supposed to be a 'not' in between 'thou shall' and 'kill.'"

"*What?*" shrieked the voice of the elderly man from earlier as the veil he had thrown over himself faded and the decoy corpse turned to dust. "I go through all this trouble to kill these people and you just let them go?"

"Well, yes," said the Ophde. "We're pacifists. What did you expect?"

"For you to kill them!" shouted the man. "Killing people in the name of pacifism isn't murder, it's pest control!"

"No," said the Ophde, glaring at the man with several thousand eyes. "It's murder. Let the innocents go, lest they come to harm."

"No," said the summoner. "This shall not stand. I shall take this to the highest authority. You are but servants, and servants must obey their masters."

"No!" blurted the Ophde. "He's not well at the moment! None may see Him, not even Mikhael!"

"No!" shouted Magus in an attempt to make it look as if he was relevant to this scene.

"Let us go," said the summoner. "You shall keep me from Him no longer."

As Magus watched, the summoner raised an iron token dangling from a chain, said a few words, and stood back as the space in front of him began to distort. The air seemed to crush in on itself, quickly spiraling into a gigantic vortex. Despite his attempts to hold on to the reality he once knew Magus was pulled in, hearing ethereal trumpeting as his sanity began to crumble.

Then, it stopped. Not suddenly, as that word is beginning to be overused, but it did stop quite rapidly. As Magus opened his eyes, he began to hyperventilate, for he saw naught but darkness. His friends were in there—the summoner and Ophanim as well—but they were all overshadowed by the environment, which was like that of the void between stars.

As the party watched, the blackness before them began to take shape, twisting and writhing as it fought to gain form. Mouths took shape and began to open, briefly attempting to speak before swirling away into the chaos, eyes pivoted in an attempt to see as much as possible before being pulled back under, and transparent cilia writhed on the surface.

"Oh Lord," said the summoner, but before he could continue, the Ophanim silenced him with a few words of power.

"What is this?" asked Magus, backing away from the chaos in horror.

"This is the Lord," said the Ophanim in a reverential tone.

"He doesn't look that godly," said Magus. "I think I'll stick with Hecate."

"He's been a bit ill," said the Ophanim.

"Does he have some kind of a cold?" asked Abda. "I assumed gods were immune to that kind of stuff."

"No," said the lead Ophde before letting out a sardonic chuckle. "Something far worse than that. Listen closely."

Magus began to listen closely, or at least stopped listening distantly.

"You understand that gods are fed via belief, and are given shape by it?"

Magus nodded. The concept was well known in wizardly circles, presumably explaining why the patron god of magic was a scantily clad woman.

"Furthermore," continued the Ophde, "You understand that belief can shift from one god to another, causing one to grow and the other to die?"

Magus yawned. He had learned most of this stuff back when he still struggled to cast magic missiles.

"Now," said the Ophde, "we have learned something new. Belief does not just go from god to god, but can also go from one part of a god to another!"

"Really?" said Magus sarcastically. "Which parts? Did his third left toe become more holy than his pinky finger?"

"You misunderstand," said the Ophde, politely ignoring the sarcasm. "Appearances, aspects of personality, even the Name itself. Those are all things that can change."

The Ophde sighed. "Our main prophet was a pacifist who talked of peace and love before the Psudorians had him nailed to a tree." After a short pause, a light flickered from one of the Ophanim's eyes, shining on the frozen form of the summoner. "We have prophets like him now. The more people believe he is vengeful, the more the Lord's condition worsens, and the more the Lord's condition worsens, the more vengeful he becomes. What was once a small pimple of darkness is now some vile cancer, changing Him before our very eyes. Can you imagine it! Being omnipotent, yet knowing you are changing and being powerless to stop it."

"Well," said Magus, "that's a nice sob story, but I still don't know what you want me to do."

Then, a rumbling sound was heard, as the maelstrom of chaos tried harder and harder to regain its shape. After a few false starts it managed to painstakingly create what was presumably meant to be a mouth, from which came a voice with the weight of a thousand eons that spoke naught but two words:

"Kill me."

"Huh," said Magus. "Is it just me or is this novel starting to get really dark?"

****

Chapter 9
For Doom the Bell Tolls

"Is there any chance of us starting this chapter without you saying 'Now what'?" asked Magus as the party walked along the dilapidated road in an attempt to put as much distance between them and the events of the previous chapter as possible.

"Given that you spoke first," responded Ærin. "The odds are pretty high."

"Stand and deliver!"

As the party looked on a group of armed men jumped out from an ambush[5] wielding blades of gleaming steel. The leader was a man wearing a brown shirt, brown pants, brown boots, and a leather jacket which was, unsurprisingly, also brown. His hair was a dirty brown, and if you can't figure out his eye color by this point, you need to work on your pattern recognition. Next to him was a dwarf wearing chain mail and a steel helm, carrying the battleaxe that seemed to be the membership card for the elusive race. Behind them was an elf with odd clothing that shimmered and changed color as he moved, although shades of green appeared to be the common denominator. A bow was slung over his shoulder, but—showing prudence generally unnoted in novels of this type—it was not yet strung.

"Oh," said the leader, noting the shiny array of cutlery displayed before him. "Sorry. I mistook you for someone else."

"Hey!" exclaimed Petrov. "I remember you! Siege of Abernackle, thirty years back! We were in an adventuring party together!"

"Petrov?" asked the leader querulously. "I heard tell you died in the raid on Carroburg."

---

[5] A type of large shrub named for its ability to hide an entire group of outlaws.

"Reports of my death were greatly exaggerated," explained Petrov. "There were some wraiths after me and I figured it would be a good idea to lay low for a while. Ærin, Magus, Abda, meet Cursor."

"Nice to meet you," said Magus.

"Likewise," responded Cursor.

"Now tell me," asked Petrov, "Where did you dig up this sorry lot?"

"Long story," said Cursor. "Let's just say the Ring of Gyges turned out to have a lot more backstory to it then we first thought. We were escorting the new Bearer to the Abyssal Plains, but the little bastard ran off. We would go after him, but others from our party were kidnapped by orcs, and we found it prudent to try and rescue them. As to our current profession, we are running short on food, and we figured that this would be the best way to replenish our supplies."

"You know what I mean," growled Petrov, glaring at the elf.

"What, him?" said Cursor. "Alithron joined us back at the council of the Magi, same as Grímsi. Don't worry; he's not with the rest of his kind."

"Oh," responded Petrov. "I see. Instead of being a spy, he's merely a Drizzit clone. Is that supposed to be any better?"

"Not really," said Grímsi, whom an astute reader will have recognized as the other dwarf. "Still, he's more tolerable than most prick-ears."

"Tell me," asked Magus. "Who is this bearer you refer to? I know of Gyges, but I did not know that anyone else had acquired the ring."

"No one much," said Cursor. "Some thief. Gangari said the midget got it from his father thirty years ago, back when they were gunning for Midgard. As to his name, I think it was Fleta. Fleto. Something like that."

"So, a Lord of the Rings parody, then?" asked Petrov. "Tell me, have you claimed the throne of Psudor yet? Has Gladius been reforged?"

"The answer to your questions," responded Cursor, "is somewhere between no and yes."

"Thank you for that cryptic answer," responded Petrov. "It's nice to see the traditions of not handing out any more plot than necessary are being kept up. Tell me, where do you head?"

"We travel to the Golden Hall," said Cursor. "The Equites require our aid. We would be going after the Bearer, but we needed to chase the orcs. It seems that those they took were slain in our absence, and it's too late to double back, so we decided to head for a new quest. Will you join us?"

"We can head with you as far as Anopolois," said Magus, "But we will have to part ways there. A detachment of the Imperial Army is heading to Minos Turris, and if we ambush them inside the city, there is a good chance of us standing victorious."

"Then let us be off."

"I'm sorry," said Magus with a smirk. "I don't have a power switch—*oh gods why are you punching me?*"

****

As night began to fall, the party began to set camp, eventually settling down in a spot along the road that presumably used to contain a wayhouse, using what remained of the furniture to start a fire. Magus and Cursor had first watch, and—as with all clichés like this one—they used it as an opportunity to talk, establish backstory, and ignoring their surroundings.

"So," said Magus, "How did you really meet Petrov? He said that you were fighting in a siege thirty years ago, and if that was true, you'd be about fifty now. "

"Eighty, actually," responded Cursor. "Being a demigod has its benefits."

"Demigod?" queried Magus. "Please explain."

"I have the blood of kings in my veins," said Cursor. "The lines of Maximus are descended from the gods themselves. Once we were many, but we now fade into darkness. One by one the Paragons have been slowly picked away, and now I am the only one left."

"Wow," said Magus. "That's deep. All I have for my backstory is one of those destroyed hometown things."

"Really?" said Cursor, obviously feigning interest. "Tell me more."

"There's really not that much to it," responded Magus. "Family killed as a child, adopted by mentor, empire attacks town, mentor dies in my arms before he can tell me something dramatic about my parents, I go on quest for vengeance, and so on, ad nauseam."

"You have been the eighth person I've met so far with that backstory," said Cursor. "I presume you have some kind of useless trinket to remind you of it."

"Close," said Magus. "I have the staff of my master. He kept alluding to it having some kind of special power, but never more than that."

"Be prepared to have it save you in the nick of time, then," responded Cursor. "Any other achievements?"

Magus chuckled sardonically. "More than you can ever imagine. I have fought that which gnaws at the roots of the world, and I have walked the Endless Stair. I have gone deep inside the bowels of the earth,[6] fighting that which slept within, but I escaped unscathed, leaving naught but corpses in my wake. There is no man on this planet who has done more than me."

"Congratulations on managing to pad your résumé then," said Cursor. "Any loot?"

---

[6] I'm sincerely wondering whether or not I should make a joke along the lines of "Dur hur hur the planet has a butthole" here.

"Some," replied Magus. "Really, other than a few medals, all I have to show for it is a magic sword that warns me when orcs are near."

"So it glows, then?" asked Cursor. "Typical."

"No," responded Magus. "It sings 'Don't Stand So Close to Me.'"

There was an awkward silence.

"Could have been worse," said Cursor. "I had one that sang 'Friday.' Melted it down for scrap first chance I got. I think it's a hubcap now."

"Really?" asked Magus. "A Friday joke? That song's old. No-one cares anymore."

"It's in the script," said Cursor. "If you've got any problems, take it up with the narrator."

Hey, it took me three years to get this published. It was topical then!

****

Dawn broke without any incursions of orcs or other beasts, and soon the party had packed up, leaving the instant the mechanics got the sun working again. After large amounts of hitchhiking, they managed to get along a few miles, but that's a bit boring, so let's skip a few weeks.

As the party approached Anopolois, Magus realized he knew nothing about the realm he was soon to enter, so he figured that it would be prudent to ask Cursor.

"I have never been to Minos Turris," said Magus. "How large is it? What is it like?"

"Greater than you can ever imagine," said Cursor with a sigh. "The city proper is built astride a towering mount which we carved into five concentric rings, each higher than the last. Atop the fifth and final level, there is a gigantic tower, containing the palace off the stewards, along with the Garden of the White Tree. However, no matter how majestic the city is, it still pales in grandeur to what we had during the days of the Tax Romana. The old capital, Rheme, was twice as large and twice as grand, but it was taken by the Gauls, forcing us to relocate."

"Who are the Gauls?" asked Magus.

"One of the tribes of feral goblins pushed from their native lands during the War of Darkness. They had nowhere else to go, so they threw themselves against our walls with ferocity the likes of which shall never be seen again. We reclaimed the capitol, but it had already been burnt to the ground, and occupation was impossible."

"Wait," said Magus. "If Rheme is Rome, and Minos Turris is Istanbul, than what's Ankhgard supposed to be?"

"Victorian London?" suggested Cursor. "I think they have clockwork, and the author probably wanted to put steampunk in here somewhere."

"I suppose that makes sense," said Magus. "When we were attacked in the woods, they had some kind of steam-powered tank. Damn thing almost killed us."

"Bastards."

"Yes."

"Tell me," said Cursor. "Will you not join us on our quest to save the Equites? There is plenty of room in our party."

"Regrettably, no," responded Magus. "I must avenge my village, even though it means my doom."

"Very well," said Cursor. "The crossroads is near, and Anopolois beckons. With that, my friends, I am afraid I must be off. Come, Grímsi. We have much work to do."

Then, as Magus watched, Cursor and his party turned to the west, walking off into the sunset. Luckily, the mechanics from earlier in the chapter had skimped on their job, as otherwise the heat would have instantly incinerated the adventurers.

****

Eventually, after several weeks of hitchhiking, the party finally managed to reach Minos Turris, only to be turned back at the gate due to a firm 'No Vagrants' policy. It did not end well.

"All right," said Magus as they walked through the smoldering wreckage of the watchtower. "I'm a bit confused as to what that was supposed to accomplish."

"We're in the city, aren't we?" said Ærin.

"Yes," replied Magus, "but there's no hope of surprising the convoy now. Why'd you have to stab that guy?"

"Does it matter?" asked Ærin. "We don't need to take the empire by surprise. You just melted a stone tower with naught but the force of your will. We don't need surprise."

"Yes, we do," responded Magus.

****

"No we don't," said Ærin as they walked through the smoldering wreckage of an Imperial convoy.

"Fine," said Magus, "but this changes nothing. We still keep a low profile. We can't afford to be seen as a serious threat."

"We *are* a serious threat," Said Ærin. "There's no reason for us to keep up this charade. Today, we take on Ankhgard. Tomorrow, we take on the world."

"Great idea," said Abda. "And best of all, it leaves us the rest of the week off."

****

"Well," said Cursor as he stepped through the wreckage of what was once the Golden Hall. "This place is a bit of a mess."

"Yes," proclaimed a deep voice, presumably belonging to the man seated on the carven throne at the far end of the hall. "That it is."

"What happened?" asked Cursor, looking to the elderly man as if he had known him for years.

"The forces of Ankhgard came," said the old man. "Trained men with blades of steel, and vile barbarians from the north, all headed by their beasts of living metal. After all of the failed wars, and many pointless raids, our military was decimated before the battle even started, and I knew that it was my fault. My people left, preparing to cower in Galea's deep, while I remained here to atone for my sins and face the doom that I brought upon us. When the army arrived, finding naught but me, they destroyed the city, but left me alive to spread a message to others."

"And what is the message?" asked Cursor.

"Run."

****

"This is Galea's Deep?" asked Grímsi. "*This* is your impenetrable fortress?"

"Yes," said the defenders' captain, now the sole remaining officer present for the beginning of the war. "Five rows of earthworks—each with a bottleneck gap so soldiers will try to push through in one spot rather than spread out and climb the walls—all defending a castle built into the end of the valley. What more do you want?"

"A defense that will actually work," responded Grímsi. "Building the back of the castle into the mountains may have saved you some time, but provides a natural ramp for the invaders. Even if they still try to get in from the front, they'll probably have a few archers shooting us in the back! Furthermore—"

Then, as if the universe itself was conspiring to stop Grímsi's rant, a horn blared, cutting through his speech.

"Prepare," said Cursor. "They come."

****

Magus coughed, his voice rattling around the carriage.

"Am I the only one who has a problem with the chapter centering on someone else?" he asked. "If they keep this up much longer there's probably going to be a group of new main characters or something."

"You are the only one," said Abda, "That will never happen. Our contract states that no replacements can be brought in, and the union would intervene if the narrator broke faith at this stage. Besides, I can't blame him for looking somewhere else. It's not like hitchhiking is very interesting."

"Yes," said Ærin, "but does it count as hitchhiking if you steal someone's carriage the instant they let you in?"

"Does it matter?" asked Magus, "It's not any more interesting. Tell me," he said conversationally, rapping on the roof, "How are things going on up there?"

"Just fine, Lord," said the driver.

"Capital!" said Magus as he looked out the rear window. "I suggest you hurry up. Those orcs seem a bit angry about you driving through their camp, and I doubt they care that we made you."

"Yes, Lord."

"Very good."

Suddenly, a voice rang out at the same time as Magus's sword started to glow blue.

"Young girl, you're out of your mind, this—"

"Great," said Magus. "Just in case my day wasn't miserable enough."

****

"Cursor," said Grímsi, "I think it would be a good idea to step away from the wall."

"Why?" said Cursor, turning away from the battlements. "What reason is there for us to flee in our moment of triumph? Run if you must, but I shall stay."

"But look!" said Grímsi, pointing out to an odd, wheeled tube in the rear of the mass of orcs and imperial soldiers squatting just outside bow range. "They have the means to destroy us all."

"Nonsense," responded Cursor. "Alithron was right. You and your kind are as cowardly as you are short. Go."

"But—" protested Grímsi before he was cut off.

"Go," said Cursor, shoving him away. "We have no need for fools here."

"Very well," said Grímsi, stomping off into the main keep with murder in his eyes.

The invaders around the tube began to shuffle away, making room for a siege engineer with a flaming torch.

"Now," said Cursor, addressing the soldiers massed along the wall. "I know that you have your doubts. However, worry not. Victory shall be ours. The time of changes is upon us, but the Prophesy is on our side. "

The engineer reluctantly brought the torch to a length of matchcord on the back of the barrel, scuttling away after setting it alight.

"Remember," said Cursor. "We have legend with us."

The sparking flame on the matchcord retreated into the barrel.

"Victory is inevitable," said Cursor, "for I am the True King!"

There was a flash.

There was a sound.

There was smoke.

There was darkness.

And then there was naught but six.

****

Panting like a bellows, Grímsi sighed as he fought to defend the entrance to the catacombs. A fool. That was what the king was. Standing up on the walls, taunting a siege weapon. He had led them all to their dooms.

"Grímsi," said the elf behind him, "I'm afraid I haven't entirely honest with you."

"Is this really the best time to confess?" shouted Grímsi as he spun his axe forward to parry a blow from a rusting blade.

"I doubt I'll ever get another chance," responded Alithron as he walked closer to the melee. "But you see..."

"Yes?" asked Grímsi. "Get on with it!"

"Well," said Alithron as he pulled out an enameled dagger, "I was never really on your side."

And then there were but five.

"Well?" said the elf, facing the newly empty doorway and raising his arms to the sky. "Hurry up. I wish to join my brothers in death."

And then there were merely four.

****

"Well," said Magus as he roasted a piece of meat over the burning remains of their coach. "That was an interesting adventure. I can't believe we made it out alive. Still, we won in the end. Anyone want a piece of orc crackling?"

"Nah," said Petrov. "I've never liked orcflesh. I spent five years behind elvish lines with nothing to eat but Soylent Green[7]. With luck, I shall never have to eat the stuff again."

"What else will you eat?" asked Magus. "The orcs destroyed our provisions."

"Rocks!" responded Petrov. "And after that, my own beard!"

****

On the crest of the mount over Galea's deep, the White Wizard mounted his horse, charging at the imperial forces with an entire platoon of Equites behind him. He managed to get halfway down the hill before he realized that the enemy was armed with pikes.

And then there were momentarily five, but soon it went back to four.

---

[7]The dwarven equivalent of beef jerky. It was called such because "flesh of the slain" gave the dwarves bad public relations. The traditional method of consumption is to leave it to soak in a bucket of water for an hour, and then eating the bucket.

Chapter 10
The Dim Lord

Ankhgard, city of cities. Enclosed by its circular wall, the realm inside was like another world. Its many smokestacks billowed dark clouds so massive they sometimes blotted out the sun, at which point the city was lit by the many sweatshops. Although several roads lead from it, their main route of trade was the Ankh, the river from which the city gets its name. Due to its proximity to the mountains, the river used to have a habit of flooding every year, but ever since the dam and adjoining reservoir had been built, the only thing the citizens had to worry about was getting mugged. In the center of all the mayhem was a tower.

After wading through the paragraph of expository detail, the party walked over to the line to enter the gate, waiting impatiently for the guards to finish peace-bonding everyone's swords and stamping everyone's papers.

"Seems like they ramped up security since the last time we were in the country," said Magus.

"Can you blame them?" responded Ærin. "The last time we were in the country we burned an entire city to the ground."

"Hey!" shouted one of the guards. "It's the insurgents! Sound the alarms!"

As soon as the guard said that, he noticed that his fellows had taken advantage of him pausing to shout, running inside the city and slamming the gates behind them.

"Hey," he shouted. "Don't leave me out here!"

At this point he ceased to say anything, not so much out of lack of need as because the approaching wizardly fireball had consumed him, along with a sizeable portion of the gate.

"*Arrgggghhhh!*" said the guard around the time his bones reached the melting point of iron.

"That was slightly overkill," said Ærin.

"And?" responded Magus. "Let's go in."

****

"If I tell you what I know," asked the quavering voice. "Will you let us live?"

"Yᴇs," responded the voice of darkness.

"Very well. We don't have what you want. The two others took it and split it back at Riverford. Can me and Pepin go now?"

The voice of darkness chuckled with the fall of empires, and even as its source swung into view, darkness fell on the other voice as well.

And then there were naught but two.

****

"Well," said Magus as he viewed the destruction he had wrought. "This seems to be working out nicely."

"Yes," said Ærin, "but-"

"Look out!" shouted Petrov.

Despite his warning, Magus barely had enough time to jump out of the way as a rock from one of the siege catapults atop the walls crashed down, pulverizing a nearby house.

"What the hell?" shouted Magus. "They're firing into their own city!"

"The empire seems to have pissed its collective pants!" shouted Abda. "Come on! Let's get to the tower! They daren't fire on that!"

"*What?*" shouted Magus, "You expect them to stop just because we hid inside the largest building in the city after they're already willing to—"

A flying bit of shrapnel from one of the more recent impacts perforated Magus's hat.

"Do you have a better idea?" asked Abda.

"No," said Magus, clearly shaken. "Lead on."

****

Two of what appear to be children, standing at the edge of a pit of flame. The taller one stands on the edge, dangling something over the chasm, while the fatter one hangs back.

"Throw it now!" shouted Fat. "Throw the ring into the fire!"

"I can't, Samuel," responded Tall. "It is a part of me!"

"It isn't!" said Fat. "It's the source of the corruption! It's killing you! I'll drop it if it comes to that!!"

"I'm sorry, Sam," replied Tall as he turned and drew his sword. "But I'm afraid I can't let you do that. Don't worry. This is for the best."

And then there could only be one.

****

"Well," said Magus after they reached the gates. "You seem to have been half right. On one hand, they stopped firing. On the other hand, judging by the thaumic radiation coming from that building, it probably contains some of the most powerful mages on the continent. Odds are they don't need siege weapons to kill us."

"*And?*" asked Ærin. "We knew killing the Emperor was going to be tough. Do you want to just back out now?"

"Of course not," responded Magus, striding into the tower. Or at least he would have done so if it weren't for all the locks and doors and things.

"All right," said Magus. "That's it. PARVA PORCO, PARVA PORCO, LICEAT INGREDI!"

As Magus spat the magic words, the doors exploded inward with such force the iron hinges were ripped in twain, and little bits of mahogany were embedded in the obsidian walls.

"Damn," said Magus as he walked past the remains of a guard who'd happened to be standing in the wrong place. "Did I do that?"

"Technically," responded Abda, "the shrapnel from the blast was what did that. However, for all intents and purposes, yes, you killed him."

"Wow," said Magus.

"Now where should we go?" asked Petrov. "It's not like they're kind enough to post maps of the place everywhere."

"Don't worry," said Magus. "Just follow my lead. SI MORIAMINI IN ELEVATOR, PLANTO CERTUS VENTILABIS QUAE SURSUS BULLA!"

A ten by ten square was instantly blasted through the roof of the room, along with those above t before turning into dust. Meanwhile, the square of floor below it began to levitate, lifting the party into the air.

"Ladies and gentlemen," snarked Magus. "Please keep your hands and feet inside the ride at all times. I heavily doubt that any of you are pregnant, but if you are, I suggest you consider abortion, as giving birth during the final boss battle would be really awkward."

****

One light, alone on the basalt rock.

A dark hand, reaching for the ring.

And now, at last, there are none.

****

As the platform flew, entire rooms and floors zoomed by, each practically a cavern in its own right. As they flashed by faster and faster, the gleaming obsidian walls blurred into shades of black.

Eventually the blur refocused as the floor slowed and stopped, sliding neatly into the penthouse floor. Stepping into the Emperor's throne room, Magus saw a granite throne ahead of him, decorated with gleaming pieces of ivory and smoked glass as dark as the void between the stars. All in all, it would have been very ominous if someone had been sitting there.

"Well," said Abda. "That was a bit of an anticlimax."

Magus was looking at a small doorway in the side of the chamber.

"Be quiet. I hear voices."

As the party crept closer, they looked inside and saw two figures wearing robes of darkest night. One was presumably the Emperor, as it was highly improbable there were two six foot tall skeletons clad in robes of the finest silk wandering around. The other was wearing rougher robes, with a mace and a short sword attached to his belt.

As Magus watched, the Emperor approached the second figure.

"Well?" asked the Emperor. "What reason do you have to be here?"

The second figure simply stared.

"*Insolence!*" shouted the Emperor. "Remember, you are no longer the Greatest of Nine. Now, you are simply the least of one."

"True," said the figure as a red light began to pulse from its cowl. "However, you have made one mistake."

"And what is that?" asked the Emperor.

"I have this," responded the figure as it extended a hand, showing the golden ring on its middle finger. "Although this is the body of the Lord of the Nine, I am not he. I am the first Dark Lord. I am Sargon!"

The Emperor gasped and kneeled.

"My Lord! I did not know you had returned."

"Of course," snapped Sargon. "That was the point. Stop your groveling. The Alliance is coming, and I need to leave for Dur Sharrukin."

"The Alliance?" asked the Emperor.

"You never were the brightest," responded Sargon. "The Artorians are coming, and those they worship with them. The fall of your empire will leave the north undefended, and with the power the Artorians will lose here, I will be able to sweep through the west as well."

As soon as Sargon had finished talking, a crash from outside the tower signaled the coming of dragons, and a brown-haired man burst through the window, landing in the center of the room. Looking from side to side, he quickly turned toward the doorway, glaring straight at Magus.

"Magus Breeman," said Aragon, as of course it was he. "Fancy meeting you here. Come to me now, and I shall give you a quick death."

"That's nice," said Sargon. "Be quiet now, the adults are talking."

"Wait," said Magus. "Who the hell are you?"

"I'm the manipulator who was secretly behind everything," said Sargon. "This is the bit where we fight and I teleport away after being defeated to provide a sense of closure while still leaving room to develop."

"Bullshit," said Magus. "There is no way the author would be stupid enough to replace the villain with some random asshole four pages before the end of the novel."

"Why not?" asked Sargon. "That's the kind of thing cliffhangers are made out of."

"Like hell they are," said Magus. "This ends now."

"We're getting a sequel out of this at the very least," responded Sargon, towering over Magus like the Colossus of Rhodes.[8] "The only way this series ends is over my dead body!"

"Terms accepted," said Magus. "YOUR MANUSCRIPT DOES NOT MEET OUR NEEDS AT THE PRESENT TIME!"

Resonating with the power of Magus's voice, a grey sphere burst into existence, expanding until it covered the whole city. When it hit the Emperor, the lights emanating from his eye sockets winked out, leaving only brittle and ancient bones that quickly crumbled to dust. When it hit Sargon his body lost substance, leaving naught but a golden ring. When it hit Aragon it stole his power, leaving him as week as a newborn kitten. When it hit the dragon flying outside, she fell out of the sky as her wings went stiff. Then it hit the foundations of the tower and did something far worse.

After all magic in the city had been dispelled, all the enchantments that allowed such large buildings to be built on tunnel-ridden loam vanished. Soon, the tower began to shudder, falling rubble smashing the houses below. This was but a minor detail relative to the crumbling of the dam, which released a flood of water into the city.

"You idiot!" shouted Ærin. "What were you thinking? This tower is going to fall, and it's taking us with it! There's no way we'll be able to climb down in time!"

"Yes," said Magus as he waved a hand glowing with magical power. "So it's a good thing we'll be taking the elevator."

---

[8] Sargon still didn't flash anyone on the river. It's not a perfect metaphor.

137

****

In the end, it was the ground itself that failed. It caved in under the tower, devouring what was once a bustling city and leaving naught but a rapidly growing lake of slurry. However, as Magus and the party watched from a nearby hill, they knew in the deepest recesses of their hearts that there was still something left.

After all, there was still an entire chapter to go.

****

Chapter 11
ONE MORE FINAL: I Need You (Not)

"Allright," said Ærin. "Now what?"

THE END.

One objectivist was harmed in the making of this novel.
Regrettably, I was unable to find more.

All similarities with any persons, living or dead, are completely
intentional. Stalin can suck it.

"Hey," said Magus. "We never addressed who my parents were! What was the point of me being an orphan if it never gets mentioned again?"

"Fine," said his master's ghost, rising up through the ground. "Your parents..."

"Yes...?"

"Your parents were douchebags. "

There was an awkward pause.

"Also, you aren't really an orphan. They just left you at my doorstep in a basket. It's kind of funny if you look at it in the right way."

There was another pause.

"So, yeah," said Sinyeï's ghost as it descended back into the ground. "I'm glad we cleared that up."

www.ingramcontent.com/pod-product-compliance
Lightning Source LLC
Chambersburg PA
CBHW060616130626
46555CB00002B/529